Angelique,

Love Always,

Coffee, Tea or Me

Rich Amooi

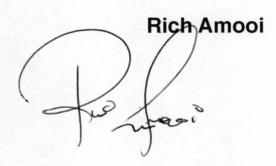

To receive updates on new releases, exclusive deals, and occasional silly stuff, sign up for Rich's newsletter at: http://www.richamooi.com/newsletter

To my sweet angel.
Without you,
none of this would be possible.

Chapter One

"No. Kissing. On. The lips!" Jack Robbins grimaced and wiped his face. "That was disgusting. Your tongue went *inside* my mouth. Do you know how distracting that is while I'm driving? Get back on your seat."

Jack glanced down at his dog, Chimichanga, who sat on his lap as they waited for the red light to change. The rescue Chihuahua didn't budge and shot him an innocent look she had perfected over the last year.

Jack shook his head. "You're lucky you're so cute, Chimi. You know that?"

Chimi agreed and licked Jack on the chin this time.

Jack pulled into the parking lot, parked the car, and scratched her on the head. "*Much* better. Kisses on the chin are perfectly acceptable. I'm also okay with cheeks and earlobes."

Jack got out of the car, tucked Chimi under his arm and walked across the parking lot toward his business, Jack's Coffee Cafe. It was the number one coffeehouse in Mountain View, California and Jack couldn't be prouder. Not only did he brew the best coffee one cup at a time, he even had a dog-friendly patio in the back.

Business was good.

So good that he'd been approached by investors to turn his cafe into a national chain.

Chimi growled at a woman who got out of her car.

"Sorry," Jack said to the woman.

Chimi had a problem with women and made it clear she wanted to be the only female in Jack's life.

He entered the back patio of his cafe and smiled. "Hey, Harvey."

"Morning, Jack." Harvey was one of his regular customers. He sat against the wall with Penzance, his Labradoodle. "How are you and Enchilada today?"

Harvey rarely called Chimichanga by her real name. The dog was going to get a complex.

Jack reached down and stroked Penzance on the head. "Another beautiful day... How are you?"

"Just Marvy."

He always was.

In fact, everyone knew him as Marvy Harvey when he had had a popular morning show on the radio back in the seventies and eighties.

Harvey folded his newspaper and set it off to the side. "I thought you had the day off."

"Todd called and said I needed to get down here ASAP. According to him, our world is falling apart."

"He can be a little dramatic."

"Tell me about it."

Like that day Todd phoned Jack and told him he was in the emergency room at General Hospital. Jack almost ran over a group of Girl Scouts as he raced to the hospital, only to find out that Todd was being treated for an ingrown toenail.

Harvey shrugged. "Well, it's a nice surprise seeing you, anyway."

Jack smiled. "Thanks. The universe likes to keep hitting us with these surprises to keep us on our toes, I guess."

"Story of my life… I thought I was going in for a routine physical exam last week and next thing you know the doctor is inserting some crazy ultrasound-thingamajig the size of a flag pole up my yahoo."

Harvey was the king of TMI.

Or maybe more accurate would be WTMI. *Way* too much information.

Jack suspected the eighty-year-old man made up his medical issues just to have something to talk about since he missed being on the radio. Harvey had a full head of white hair, but was in amazing shape for his age.

"You ever have back spasms?" asked Harvey.

"Can't say that I have."

Harvey reached down and stroked Chimi's smooth cream coat. "You will when you get to be older than dirt like me." Harvey gestured toward the cafe. "Looks like you're wanted."

Jack cranked his head around to look through the cafe

window. Todd stood inside with his hands on his hips and a *get-your-butt-in-here-now* look on his face.

He handed Chimi's leash to Harvey. "I'll be back."

"You know I'm not going anywhere. Especially with these shingles and shin splints."

Jack entered the cafe and headed toward Todd who was behind the counter, restocking the cups. The place was packed as usual and the energy was electric.

He slid behind the counter and came up behind Todd.

Todd whipped around and gave Jack another look. "Follow me."

"Can I grab a cup of coffee first?"

"This can't wait." Todd circled around the counter and walked toward the front door.

"Okay…" said Jack to himself. "I'm just the owner of the place, so don't worry about it."

What was the big mystery?

Probably nothing at all.

Jack passed by a few more regulars, said hello, and exited through the front door. He took a seat on the bench out front and watched Todd pace back and forth on the sidewalk. Todd was wearing his favorite employee t-shirt that said, "Jack's Coffee. Freshly brewed one cup at a time." It was like the other employees' t-shirts, but he insisted on the color black to distinguish himself from the employees who wore the same shirt but in hunter green.

Jack checked his watch. "I should be at home reading on

the back patio right now. What's the problem?"

Todd pointed. "*That* is the problem."

Jack stood and followed the direction of Todd's finger toward the place next door. Two workers were up on ladders installing a sign.

He backed up a few steps to read the sign. "Susie's Tea & Scones…"

This was news to him. He'd been wondering who was going to take over the place since the bakery went out of business six months ago. All the windows had been covered with paper to keep everyone from looking in while the construction workers worked inside.

Jack turned back toward Todd, not understanding what the big deal was. "I don't see the problem."

"Excuse me?" Todd took a couple of steps toward Jack and leaned in. "Twenty percent of our sales come from tea. *That's* the problem. Neither of us needs a calculator to know how much money that is."

It was *a lot* of money, that was for sure. But Jack didn't get why Todd was so concerned. He didn't consider Susie's tea shop—or any tea shop, for that matter—competition. They probably served a different kind of tea that required you to extend your pinkie finger outward as you drank it.

That wasn't competition at all.

He did admire the business savvy of the person who bought the place. They were smart to find a place that already had baking ovens, which would save them tens of thousands of dollars. Obviously, this Susie person was well educated and knew business. Still . . .

It was just tea and scones.

Jack shrugged. "I'm not worried about this place. Can I go now?"

"Well, *I* think her place could be a gold mine and we not only could lose some tea business, but maybe even some of our regular coffee drinkers."

Jack snorted. "Who would be crazy enough to switch from the bold, aromatic, sensual experience of coffee to sipping boring, perfume-infested, leafy hot water? And scones? What an absurd idea for a business."

"Wrong. Women love scones. Remember I wanted to add them to the menu a year ago?"

"I don't remember."

"Yes, you do. And did you listen? No."

A woman walked by and eyed Susie's sign. "How wonderful! I love scones."

"Me, too!" said her male companion. "We'll have to come back when they open."

Todd watched the couple walk away and then gave Jack a look. "Even *men* like scones. Go figure."

Jack studied the sign again. Could he be wrong about this? Was it possible that Susie's place could be competition?

Todd perked up. "I think that's Susie over there. I saw her going in and out of the building a few times."

"Where?"

Todd gestured with his head toward the corner. "Over there."

Jack turned and caught a glimpse of Susie as she bent over to pick up a piece of paper she dropped. She stood back up and looked in Jack's direction. They locked eyes for a moment and then he casually looked away. He didn't want her to think he was checking her out. But Jack did get a chance to admire Susie's auburn hair and pretty face before she disappeared around the corner.

Todd pointed toward her front door. "Okay, it's a good time to go check out her place."

"Do I look like a spy to you?"

"You're not spying. It's called curiosity. And based on her past behavior, she won't return from wherever she keeps going to for another twelve minutes."

"You have her under surveillance?"

"No!" Todd shrugged. "Maybe…"

Jack looked over at her front door that was propped open. He *was* curious, no doubt about that. Maybe it wouldn't hurt to have a quick look. What's the worst that could happen? They would just ask him to leave, right?

He glanced over at Susie's place again and sighed. "Okay, I'll be right back." Jack took a deep breath and walked next door. He quickly sneaked underneath the two men on the ladders without them noticing.

Once inside, he froze.

"Holy crap," he mumbled to himself, unable to believe

what he was seeing.

He glanced around the room and admired every inch of Susie's place, as if he were in a museum. There were cozy booths, tables, floor cushions, private romantic corners, candles, statues, water fountains, and bright, colorful tapestries.

"This place is amazing," he said to himself. "Huh…"

It was like an exotic blend of Morocco, India, and Thailand, with a cool modern vibe. It was so inviting and peaceful he wanted to sit and relax for a while.

Susie was a genius.

This woman had a degree in Take No Prisoners. Susie's Tea and Scones was out of this world and it wasn't even open yet. Jack didn't like the feeling in his gut.

Maybe she *was* going to be competition.

He turned to admire the beautiful mural of the Taj Mahal on the entire wall that separated Susie's business from Jack's business. In front of the wall was a giant Buddha. His eyes traveled from one side of the mural to the other and then stopped.

"What the hell?"

He moved closer and squatted, inspecting the power sockets near the floorboard. They were completely overloaded. He looked around at the numerous lamps, fountains, and other gadgets. Almost all the power cords led back to the same sockets.

"Not good…"

Jack knew from his research before moving into his own building that the overload could easily result in overheating and potentially a fire. Plus the exposed, energized terminals were a shock hazard. Jack counted at least three building code violations, plus a serious fire hazard. The last thing he wanted was for someone to get hurt or killed, plus a fire could burn right through the wall and take out his business, too.

Not gonna happen.

He would definitely warn Susie and make sure she fixed it ASAP.

Jack stood to leave, clipping the giant Buddha with the outside of his right knee.

"Oh, God."

The Buddha wobbled, ready to tip over. He reached out to grab it and ended up losing his balance, toppling over it. Jack slammed into the floor, with the Buddha landing directly on top of him. His leg swung out, kicking a colorful hand-blown floor vase, knocking it over and shattering it. He wondered if the moisture on his leg was from water in the vase or blood from his shin.

The pain was there. Lots of it.

At least the Buddha didn't break.

"What the hell are you doing?" said a man, entering the room. He stared down at Jack on the floor with the Buddha on top of him. "You got some sort of perverted Buddha fetish?"

"Don't be ridiculous. I was—"

"Give me the Buddha before you suffer the karmaquences."

Jack extended his arms upward and handed the Buddha to the man. Then he rolled over onto his knees before standing up.

The man set the Buddha off to the side. "What are you doing in my building?"

Jack stared at him for a moment. "*Your* building? You're Susie?"

"Do I *look* like a Susie to you? I'm Kenneth."

He must have been Susie's husband. A good-looking guy for sure, around thirty-five, well-built, well-groomed, well-dressed. Almost too well done up.

Maybe he was gay and *not* Susie's husband.

The man huffed and stuck his chest out. "Why are you looking at me that way?"

"Sorry. I just thought… Nothing. Let me know how much the vase was and I'll cut you a check. I'm Jack Robbins. I own the business next door."

"Is this how you normally welcome people to the neighborhood? Breaking into their businesses and then molesting the decor?" He pointed to Jack's crotch. "You pissed your pants."

Jack looked down at the giant wet spot on his pants. "It's water from the vase."

Kenneth smirked. "Sure it is."

Jack turned and pointed to the overloaded sockets near the bottom of the mural. "By the way, that right there is a fire *and* shock hazard."

Kenneth glanced over at the wall and shook his head. "Don't worry about that—I'll take care of it."

"You better because—"

"I said I'd take care of it. I'll also get you a broom."

Jack just stared at him.

"You don't expect me to clean up this mess, do you?"

Jack surveyed the pieces of glass that were scattered on the floor. "Uh, well. No. I guess not."

Just like that, Kenneth disappeared into the back room. Jack tried to wipe his pants dry with the bottom of his shirt before Kenneth came back, but the wet spot wasn't going away. He rubbed the spot harder, just as Kenneth returned with a broom and a dustpan.

"Can't leave you alone for even a minute, can I?" Kenneth said.

Jack stopped rubbing the crotch of his pants and felt his face heat up. "I was just trying to get it off."

"Looked more like you were trying to get it *on*."

Jack held out his hand. "Very funny. Just give me the broom."

Kenneth handed him a few towels. "Make sure you dry it, too." He leaned the broom and dustpan against the wall and walked away again.

Unbelievable.

Not that long ago, Jack was home relaxing on his day off. Now he was cleaning the neighbor's floor.

After he finished Jack looked around for Kenneth, but he was nowhere to be found.

"Hello?" he called. "Are you still here?"

He waited for a few seconds but there was no answer.

Jack set the dustpan off to the side, leaned the broom against the wall and limped outside. He glanced up at the sign again.

Susie's Tea & Scones

"Susie," Jack said to himself. "Looks like I need to keep an eye on you."

Chapter Two

Susie McKenna opened the large cardboard box on the counter and smiled as she pulled out containers of loose-leaf tea. Citrus Lavender Sage, Egyptian Chamomile, Gunpowder Green, Kashmiri Chai.

She loved them all.

"The competition next door is spying on us," said her brother, Kenneth. He placed some candles on the tables. "I also caught him dry-humping the Buddha."

Susie laughed. "Right." She neatly aligned the tea containers on the display shelf, making sure they were all one behind the other.

"Seriously. He was in here snooping around when you left to get more things from storage."

Susie stopped and looked up. "Jack Robbins was here?"

Kenneth arched an eyebrow. "I shouldn't be surprised you know his name."

"No, you shouldn't. You're the one who spoon-fed me information about every business within a five-mile radius."

"And because of that *you* are a well-prepared business owner."

"This is true."

Kenneth had spent over three weeks researching the neighborhood, the businesses, the owners, the demographics of the people who frequented the area, their average annual salaries, their education, median home prices, neighborhood walkability, crime reports, etc. She wouldn't be surprised if Kenneth even knew everyone's blood type.

She appreciated his business skills, but she was quite the opposite when it came to business and decisions in general. She always listened to her gut before making a move. It was usually right.

Kenneth pointed toward the corner of the room. "He also broke the blue and green Murano vase."

"Oh, no." Susie looked in the direction of where she had put the vase earlier and noticed it wasn't there anymore. Just a broom and dustpan leaning against the wall. "I *loved* that vase. How did he break it?"

"I have no idea. I was in the back when I heard the crash."

That meant she had to find a replacement vase, another thing to add to the to-do list. Normally, that wouldn't be such a big deal, but there were only three days until the grand opening and there was still so much to do.

"Don't worry," continued Kenneth. "I already ordered a replacement and paid extra to have it here tomorrow. I'm going to give him the bill too."

Susie sighed. "Good. Thanks for taking care of that."

Kenneth was a lifesaver. And he was certainly the best

choice Susie could have made for a business partner. He'd always been so supportive.

Well, not always.

Kenneth wasn't the best brother in the world as a child.

He was hell with a penis.

She cried when he set her Garden Party Barbie on fire.

She cried when he smashed her face into the cake on her tenth birthday.

He used to hide under a blanket and pretend he was the voice of her Teddy Ruxpin doll, telling her that if she fell asleep, a ten-legged hippopotamus would crash through her bedroom wall and take a giant crap on her.

But that was then, and this is now.

Kenneth was the best brother in the world and more than qualified to be a business partner. Good thing Susie ignored the advice she read online regarding going into business with a family member.

Speaking of business, she wondered why Jack was in her building. Was he really spying on her?

She tossed the empty cardboard box on the floor behind her. "Did Jack say why he stopped by?"

Kenneth shook his head. "We never got around to a normal conversation. I handed him a broom and told him to sweep up the mess he made."

Susie's mouth hung open, looking back over toward the broom and dustpan. "Tell me you didn't really do that."

"Of course I did!"

"God, Kenneth. He probably thinks you're a jerk."

Kenneth laughed. "No, he thought *I* was *you*. He asked me if I was Susie! Can you believe that crap?"

Susie laughed. "Now *that* is funny."

He shook his head. "Not funny at all."

"Well, a broken vase is not the end of the world. Let's take a break and eat something."

Kenneth brushed off his hands and smiled. "Mexican again?"

Susie nodded. "You know me well."

They headed up Castro Street toward Los Charros. Her favorite Mexican dish was chicken enchiladas, but today a cheese quesadilla with some chips and salsa sounded perfect. They'd been working hard all morning and still had a lot to do, but she needed to eat.

Susie grabbed Kenneth's arm in front of Jack's place and pulled him to a stop. "Hang on a second."

She moved closer and peeked through Jack's front window. His cafe was packed. Obviously the man knew how to run a business. His customers looked happy and there was a decent line of people ordering. Out of curiosity, she searched the tables, looking for mugs with dangling tea bags and saw a few.

Kenneth chuckled. "Now *you're* spying on the competition?"

"He's not competition, and I'm just looking." She gestured to the tall man wearing the black Jack's t-shirt. "Is that Jack?"

Kenneth inched closer to Susie to look inside. "No. I don't know who that guy is. Looks like a supervisor. Let's go —I'm hungry."

Another man appeared behind the counter.

Susie pulled Kenneth back again. "What about him?"

Kenneth let out a deep breath and looked in again. "Yup. That's him. Pervert."

Susie nodded and admired the owner of the coffee business. It was the guy who was watching her earlier on the sidewalk when she dropped her to-do list.

He was tall and slim. He had medium-length, wavy, brown hair that wasn't too short and not too long. He wore jeans and a black v-neck t-shirt that complemented his upper body. Not a huge guy. Just enough muscle to show he was in shape. He exuded confidence, which she liked.

"Are you undressing him with your eyes?" asked Kenneth.

Susie turned to Kenneth. "Stop it." She looked back inside just as the man next to Jack pointed in her direction.

Jack turned and locked eyes with Susie, just like they had done this morning.

She held his gaze. "I think I'd like to have some fun with Jack."

"Jacuzzi party?"

"Don't be ridiculous." Susie smiled. "I'm talking about right here, right now. Follow my lead."

"I don't like that devious look on your face."

"I was going for playful, not devious. I need to work on that." She pulled out a pen and pad from her purse and looked back inside the cafe. She nodded and pretended to write a few things on the paper. "Point to something inside the cafe."

Kenneth did a double take. "What?"

"We're pretending here. Point to something *inside* Jack's place. Anything. Then say a few random words about whatever you point to. Come on—play along."

Kenneth sighed and pointed to the brick wall inside. "That's a brick wall. The bricks are red. There are lots of red bricks on the red brick wall."

"You sound like Dr. Seuss." She pretended to write a few sentences and then eyed Jack, who hadn't taken his eyes off Susie. She did her best to keep a straight face.

Men were so easy to play with.

She air-scribbled a few more words on the notepad, nodded like she was deep in thought, and stuck the pad and pen back in her purse. "That should do it. Let's go."

They turned to continue up Castro Street when she heard a male voice from behind them. "Excuse me!"

That was easier than she thought.

Susie removed the grin from her face and turned around as Jack approached her.

"You're in trouble now," Kenneth whispered.

"I didn't do anything," Susie whispered back. She sent

an innocent smile in Jack's direction. "Yes?"

Jack looked at Kenneth for a moment and then got his eyes back on Susie. "Can I help you with anything?"

"Oh. No, thanks. Just looking…" Susie turned to walk away, knowing there was no way he would let the conversation end like that.

"I'm Jack Robbins."

She stopped and turned around again, giving him her best look of confusion. "Pardon me?"

He pointed to the Jack's Coffee Cafe sign in the window. "I'm Jack Robbins—this is my place. Are you Susie?"

"I am." Susie gestured to her building with her head. "And *that* is *my* place."

Jack nodded, looking like a kid who had been stumped by a long word in a national spelling bee competition. "Okay… Did you have a question about something? I mean, about my business?"

Susie played up the theatrics as if she had missed part of the conversation. "I'm not sure what you mean. Why would I have a question?"

Jack pointed back over his shoulder with his thumb toward his cafe. "It's just…I saw you looking in my window and taking notes, so…" He shrugged. "I assumed you were curious about something."

She shook her head. "No. Not at all. I wasn't taking notes."

Jack blinked twice. He casually looked down at her purse

and then lifted his gaze back up to Susie. "You weren't taking notes?"

"No. Just looking. Kenneth was fascinated with your red brick wall." She elbowed Kenneth. "Weren't you, Kenneth?"

"Huh? Oh...yeah. Very fascinated. It's so...red...and bricky."

Susie turned her attention back to Jack. "What about you? Did you have any questions for me?"

He stared at her for a moment, his eyes shooting back and forth between Susie and Kenneth. "Why would I have questions?"

She shrugged. "I don't know. I heard you stopped by for a little visit. Kenneth told me you're *very* fond of Buddhas."

Jack's face turned red, and he shifted back and forth from one leg to the other.

Poor guy.

He looked across the street toward East West Bookshop, probably trying to buy some time as he figured out how to respond to her. Either that or he was wondering what types of Buddhas they had in stock.

He finally turned back toward Susie and jammed his hands in his pockets. "Sorry about that. I guess curiosity got the best of me. And I'll pay for the broken vase." He eyed her purse again. "Okay, I guess I should get back inside. I assume Kenneth told you about your electrical problem."

"No." She turned to Kenneth and raised an eyebrow. "What problem?"

Kenneth waved off the topic. "Don't worry about it. I've got it covered."

"Good," Jack said. "Just take care of it soon because it's a violation of the—"

"I told you. I've got it covered."

Jack gave Kenneth a look.

Kenneth gave the look right back to Jack.

They looked like two bighorn sheep in the wild, getting ready to head butt each other.

But which one would make the first move? Or would one of them give in and walk away?

"Okay then…" Jack said, taking the high road. He turned to her. "Nice to meet you, Susie."

"You too."

Susie and Kenneth continued down the street past Crepevine and made a left toward Los Charros. Susie crinkled her nose. "It seemed like a fun idea at the time, but I admit I feel a tad bit guilty about doing that."

"You should."

"Great. Rub it in."

Susie was happy to have her brother close by again, even when he made her feel guilty. They both had moved to North Carolina to be closer to their parents. After a couple of failed relationships, Susie needed a fresh start and moved back to California. It always felt like home to her.

Kenneth had his own bad luck with the opposite sex. After his divorce was final he'd decided to move back to

California as well, to be close to Susie. That was when they'd come up with the idea of opening a tea shop. Kenneth knew a lot about business and accounting, so it was a perfect match.

Kenneth's biggest flaw was thinking he could do everything. He would rather try to solve any problems himself and save the money. Susie believed in hiring professionals for everything. Yes, Kenneth had saved her a lot of money while trying to open up the business. But if you don't do things right the first time, it will end up costing you more in the long run.

Speaking of which…

"What's the problem with the electrical Jack mentioned?"

Kenneth waved off her question. "Nothing I can't handle."

So predictable.

As they entered Los Charros and grabbed a table by the window, her thoughts drifted back to her good-looking neighbor next door. It was cute how Jack was worried about what she had written on the notepad. He had nothing to worry about. Their businesses were completely different and there were plenty of customers for everyone. Hopefully he was smart enough to know they weren't competitors. Then again, he was a man.

And men had egos.

Big egos.

Chapter Three

Three days later Jack stared through the window at the long line outside his cafe door. It was so long it almost reached the corner. Business was very good.

Too bad they weren't his customers.

Susie's grand opening was in full swing next door and Mountain View was buzzing with excitement. Everyone was talking about her amazing, unique place. He had to admit she did an outstanding job preparing for the grand opening, but he still wondered why people were so excited about tea and scones.

"Not good," said Todd, scooting up next to Jack and eyeing the line outside. "We're not going to hit our numbers this month if this continues."

Jack sighed. "It's been one day. People are curious—no big deal. Grand openings tend to draw the big crowds when there are free samples, but soon the excitement fades and you find out what the business is really made of."

Todd didn't look so convinced. "I think Susie's on to something. She found a hole in the market and filled the gap. I wouldn't be surprised if she spurred a movement of more tea houses opening in the area."

"Tea is tea and coffee is coffee. Two different beasts."

"If you say so."

Susie appeared on the sidewalk, talking to customers in line and carrying a tray of scone samples. She was good—working the line like a politician. For a grand opening she looked as cool as ice. Almost like she had done this before.

Jack glanced around at his cafe. It was the first time in a while since he'd seen multiple open seats and tables. Typically, his place was packed all day long. Even some of his regulars were missing. Probably just a coincidence. No way Harvey would be in that line. The man lived on coffee and—

Todd smacked Jack in the arm and pointed to the middle of the line. "Look. There's Harvey in Susie's line." He shook his head in disgust. "Traitor."

Jack couldn't believe it. The man who he thought would be the last person on earth to go next door was waiting in Susie's line.

Jack wiped his hands on a towel and hung it back on the rack. "I'll be back."

"That's right. Put him in his place. Tell him if he tries her tea he's not allowed in here anymore. And neither is Penzance."

"Don't be ridiculous. Harvey's a good guy and Penzance is Chimi's best friend. I'm not going to ban them from the place just because he's curious about Susie's new business. However, I will find out what he's up to."

Jack headed outside and slowly opened the door, careful

not to bang it into the people standing directly in front of it. He slid between two women chatting about how excited they were to try the scones. Harvey saw Jack coming and turned away, almost like he wanted to hide.

"Hey, Harvey."

Harvey turned around to face Jack, pretending to be surprised Jack was there. "Oh, hey! How's it going, Jack?"

Jack surveyed the crowd and nodded. "Good. I didn't know you were a fan of tea."

He leaned in. "It's not so much the tea. She's giving away *free* scones and Marian used to make me scones all the time! You know my teeth are made of sugar cane." He slapped Jack on the back and leaned in. "It's easy to become a fan of anything when it's free. I'll be back at your place tomorrow, as usual. Don't you worry."

"I'm not worried about it."

Susie approached with a smile on her face that briefly paralyzed Jack. He quickly dropped his gaze to the sidewalk, pretending to look for something.

Susie looked down toward the cement. "Did you lose something, Jack?"

Just my dignity. "No. Not at all."

She held the tray of scone samples in his direction and smiled again. "Care to try a sample of my freshly baked scones?"

"That's okay. Thank you."

"Oh, come on. Try one."

Her smile was a breath of fresh air. It relaxed him but at the same time made him worry about why he was enjoying her smile so much.

Knock it off. She's the enemy.

"Come on," Susie said, pushing the tray closer to Jack.

There was that smile again.

Harvey reached in front of Jack. "Don't mind if I do!" He grabbed four pieces of the scones from the platter and popped the first sample in his mouth. "Oh my God, I've died and gone to Heaven—a heaven filled with the most delectable scones. This is going to wreak havoc on my high cholesterol, but I don't give a damn." He ate another one and moaned.

Jack eyed the plate of small bite-sized samples and wrinkled his nose. "What kind are they?"

"Live a little. Take one and pop it in your mouth."

Jack was impressed. She was a good salesperson. Not one of many words, but she had a down-to-earth confidence he liked. He wrinkled his nose again and reached for a small piece of scone, putting it in his mouth. He chewed slowly, not expecting to be that thrilled with it.

That's where he was wrong.

The scone was amazing—soft on the inside, crunchy on the outside.

He eyed the platter as he finished chewing.

Susie laughed and pushed the tray in his direction. "Yes, you can have another."

Jack grabbed another small piece and cleared his throat. "Not bad."

"Uh-huh. Not bad. You're drooling."

Jack wiped his mouth. "Okay. They're...tasty. You made these?"

"Of course I made them."

He shrugged. "You never know. You could have gotten them from Safeway or Costco."

"If my grandmother heard you compare her scone recipe to the scones from a supermarket, you'd be dead right now."

Jack let out a nervous chuckle. "Sorry. I'm just surprised. They're good." He reached for another piece. "Okay, they're great."

"You got *that* right."

Jack watched Susie as she moved away, handing out samples to other people in the line. He had no idea why it was so difficult to pay her a compliment. It's not like admitting she had a better business or anything. She had great scones, end of story.

"She's a looker," Harvey blurted out. "Don't you think?"

Jack turned and checked her out. She was attractive all right.

She must have some serious willpower not to eat those scones all day because her figure was slim and curvy in the all the right places. She wore blue jeans and a purple t-shirt that said, *Susie's*. He glanced down at his own t-shirt that said, *Jack's*. Her eyes were the same color as the dark walnut chest in his bedroom.

"Earth to Jack."

Jack took his focus off Susie and turned back to Harvey. "Yeah. She's a looker for sure."

Not that it really mattered. She was obviously married, even though Jack wasn't sure what Susie was doing with a guy like Kenneth. He was way too serious and didn't seem to take the warning about the code violations seriously. Speaking of which...

Jack made his way toward Susie's tea shop and peeked inside the window. He just wanted to make sure Kenneth took care of the problem. There were so many people inside he couldn't get a good look at the mural. He turned back and saw Susie down near the corner, engaged in a lively conversation with an older woman.

He entered her place and made his way to the mural. He glanced down toward the floor where he had spotted the code violations a few days earlier. There were now a few potted cactus plants in the same spot. Maybe they did fix the code violations.

Good.

He turned to leave but then decided to stop and look behind the pots to be sure.

That's when he got the big surprise.

"Unbelievable," he mumbled to himself.

They hadn't fixed the problem.

The overloaded sockets and the exposed energized terminals were exactly the same as the other day. They hadn't even considered fixing the problem. Not only was it unacceptable, it was plain wrong, against the law, and dangerous.

And they thought they could just cover up the problem or hide it?

Wrong.

He turned and ran straight into the chest of Kenneth.

"Spying again, Jack?"

Jack turned and pointed to the cables on the floor behind the pots. "I thought you said you were going to take care of that."

"I am."

Jack blinked. "This year?"

Kenneth crossed his arms and sighed. "As you can tell we have a big week going on here. The grand opening is more important than a little electrical problem."

"*Little* electrical problem?"

"Look, we don't need to be discussing this right now. So unless you're here to ask the Buddha out on a date, I would recommend going back to your place and worrying about things on your side of the wall."

Jack gave Kenneth a look and slid by him without saying another word. Now he was pissed.

He pulled the door open and Susie entered with an empty tray.

Rich Amooi

She jerked her head back, surprised to see him. "More scones? Just a second and I'll get you some."

"That's quite alright. And your husband has a serious attitude problem."

"Husband? But I'm not—"

Jack walked out before she could finish her sentence. No use staying there and chitchatting if they weren't going to take him seriously. The line outside was even longer than before. The inside of his cafe was like a ghost town. This wasn't good. And to top it off they were putting his property in jeopardy with the shock and fire hazards.

If they weren't going to do something about it, he would.

Once back in his office he went online and found the phone number for the local government office he needed. A few seconds later, he dialed the number.

"City inspector's office," the woman answered.

"I'd like to file a complaint against a business who has several building code violations. They have potential shock and fire hazards."

"All complaints must be made in writing."

"Seriously?"

"You can find the form to print on our website. Fill it out completely and mail it to us."

"I can't just report them over the phone?"

"I'm sorry, sir. No."

"Can I fill out the form and then drop it off in person?"

"No, sir. All reports must arrive in the mail and must

30

have an official postage stamp with a date."

"Who uses the mail anymore?"

"We do, sir."

Jack sighed. "And what happens if a business burns down because you didn't process the complaint in time?"

"That would be a different form, sir."

Jack stared at the phone for a moment. "Fine. Thank you."

He hung up and shook his head. The city department was still living in the prehistoric ages, obviously. But he wasn't going to let that stop him. He printed the form from their website and filled it out, mentioning every single violation he saw at Susie's. After he finished, he stuck it in an envelope and stuck a stamp on it, setting it off to the side.

He stared at the envelope for a moment.

He wasn't overreacting, was he?

No way.

It was the right thing to do, and it had nothing to do with his slow day in sales.

This wasn't personal.

He left his office and joined Todd behind the counter. "How are we doing?"

Todd frowned. "We're down thirty percent compared to last week."

If Jack could be sure this would only last a couple days, it would be no big deal. But if people started frequenting Susie's place on a regular basis, he was in trouble. No way he could sustain that type of hit to the income for too long. That would also mean a big fat *no* from the investors when it came to turning his cafe into a national chain.

How could things have changed so quickly?

"I had visions of retiring at the age of forty," Todd said. "Buying a boat and sailing around the world like Christopher Cross."

"You mean Christopher Columbus?"

"No. Christopher Cross. You know the song 'Sailing,' don't you? Never mind. I'd be perfectly happy with a Tesla and a beach house. My point is I will not allow my dreams to be shattered. We need to do something."

"Like what?"

Todd perked up. "I'm glad you asked!"

Chapter Four

The next day, Susie stared through her shop window at the line outside of Jack's cafe.

"Unbelievable," she mumbled to herself.

Jack had the nerve to give away free cups of tea with any pastry purchase.

She had wondered why it was so slow on her second day of business. It's not like she expected it to be as busy as the first day, but she had thought the steady stream of curious people would keep coming by for a while. Then the big community festival would expose her business to thousands more.

What Jack did was wrong.

Fortunately, she didn't let things like these get to her. She had a strong mind and knew the negative thoughts would get her nowhere.

She closed her eyes and took a deep breath.

Better.

Now it was time to come up with her own promotion.

Lucky for Susie that Jack ran out of pastries after a few hours and had to stop the promotion. People trickled back into her shop and by the late afternoon business was amazing again. Still, she had to watch out for Jack and had to be prepared for his shenanigans.

After she locked up, she walked past Jack's cafe as he came out.

Jack threw her a cocky grin. "Hey, neighbor."

The guy had the nerve to pretend he did nothing wrong.

"Hi, Jack. How was business today?"

"Outstanding." He locked the front door and turned toward her, smiling. "Best day of the week, actually. And you?"

"Good. Although I was quite surprised you gave away cups of tea. Have you ever done that before?"

"No! It just came to me."

"Just came to you…"

"Yeah. Well, one of my employees came up with it and I thought it was a great idea. Oh… I hope you don't think this had something to do with you."

"Why would I think that?"

He shrugged. "I don't know. You sell tea, you know?"

"Yes, I'm *well* aware I sell tea." And she knew it had *everything* to do with her, but she wasn't going to say a word. "You have any promotions scheduled for tomorrow?"

"Not sure yet. You?"

She smirked. "I guess you'll have to wait and see." She continued down the street, Jack walking right behind her.

"What do you have planned?" Jack asked.

"Who said I had something planned?"

"You didn't say you didn't."

"I didn't say I did."

Susie continued walking, and he kept pace with her.

He smiled as they walked side by side. "Looks like we're going in the same direction."

She kept her eyes on the sidewalk ahead of her and continued to walk. "It seems so…"

She headed down the street past a few more buildings when they both stopped in front of the Mountain View Chamber of Commerce.

"Oh…" Jack glanced at Susie and pointed to the front door. "You going in here?"

"I am. And you?"

"Yeah…"

They stared at each other for a long moment until Susie pointed toward the door. "It's the round handle there. Twist it and the door opens. Like magic."

"Okay…" Jack opened the door and waved Susie through. "After you. Please."

"Thank you."

They were being formal at the moment, but it felt to Susie like they were playing a game. What type of game she wasn't sure.

Jack followed Susie through the hallway to the conference room in the back. He pointed toward the door again. "Don't tell me you're going in here too."

"I am. And you?"

Jack nodded and opened the door, waving Susie through again. "Okay, then. Please, after you…"

"Thank you."

He followed her inside and closed the door behind them. Six people sat around the large mahogany conference table in the middle of the room, all engaged in conversation.

"Great!" said Dave Blatt, president of the Mountain View Chamber of Commerce. He stood and held out his hand to Susie. "Nice to see you again, Susie. I see you've already met Jack—not a surprise since you're neighbors. Grab a seat and we'll get started!"

Jack and Susie glanced at each other and took a seat in the two empty chairs. After introductions were made to the other board members, the meeting began.

Susie had no idea Jack had also volunteered to be part of the downtown festival planning committee and hoped there wouldn't be any issues. After that stunt he pulled today, she didn't trust the man and would be on full alert. And if he had a problem with her being on the committee, too bad.

Dave pointed to the two words on the whiteboard and underlined them.

Fresh Ideas.

He smiled and rubbed his hands together. "Okay… Today, I wanted to cover a few things. Jack and Susie graciously volunteered to help at the last minute. Just about everything is in place for the festival, but we still feel like something's missing. Like we can make it even better…

We've pretty much done the same thing year after year, so it's not a surprise the attendance numbers have been going down. We'd like to shake it up a little and get some of those people back, plus we want to draw fresh new blood to the festival. Increasing attendance is our biggest goal this year, so I'd like everyone to put their heads together for some brainstorming to see if we can come up with something else to add to the line-up."

Susie raised her hand.

Dave chuckled. "We're not so formal here, Susie, but I appreciate your enthusiasm. Everyone can just jump in to share anything."

Susie nodded. "Great. I went through the PDF of the program for last year's festival and was curious why there wasn't any live music."

Dave scratched the side of his face. "That's a good question. How come we haven't had live music? Jack?"

Jack shrugged. "Well, you weren't president at the time, but we decided that the music was too much of a distraction. We want people to come and socialize, sample the food, and enjoy the festive mood. Blasting music at them would only annoy them, making it harder to have a conversation."

Susie sat forward in her chair. "Well. Nobody said anything about blasting music."

"Live music is loud."

"I wasn't talking about bringing in The Rolling Stones."

Jack laughed. "The Rolling Stones? How old are you?"

"What does that have to do with anything?"

He could make fun of her and her reference to The Rolling Stones all he wanted. She didn't care. Susie admitted she loved the same music her mother used to listen to while she cleaned the house on the weekends. The Eagles. Fleetwood Mac. Journey. Billy Joel. Elton John. Bruce Springsteen. The older music seemed to have more meaning, more depth. Not like so much of the music these days filled with angst or talking about hooking up.

Dave cleared his throat. "Okay, we're already getting off track here—just a moment." He opened a document on his laptop and scrolled down, taking his time to read something. "The attendance numbers from the second year were bigger than the first year, so people didn't have a problem with the live music or they wouldn't have returned. I think bringing back the live music is a *great* idea, but is it possible with such short notice?"

"It doesn't hurt to try," Susie said, trying to stay positive.

Dave smiled. "Good point! If we're not able to get a band, we're right where we were, nothing lost. I think we should try to make it happen. All in favor?"

All hands went up, including Jack's, although his was the last.

"Great!" said Dave, pumping his fist in the air. "Susie, since you mentioned it do you mind looking into some local bands for us?"

"I'd be happy to."

The room suddenly seemed smaller.

Maybe because Jack's ego was taking up so much space.

Susie could feel the glare of her neighbor, but avoided looking in his direction.

<<<>>>

Jack stared at Susie and wondered who the hell this woman was. He should have opened his mouth when Dave asked for suggestions. He wasn't sure why he contradicted Susie since he had thought of bringing live music back for the festival as well. But *she* said it first. They wouldn't believe him if he said he had thought of the same thing.

Susie raised her hand again. "Oops. Sorry." She dropped her hand back down.

Dave chuckled. "No problem. You thought of something else?"

She nodded. "What if we got a celebrity to be the Master of Ceremonies?"

Dave chuckled. "I love this idea since *I'm* the one who has to make those announcements. I would much rather be making the rounds, checking in with everyone and making sure everything is going according to plan. Once again, this is a big-ticket item and we don't have a lot of time to make it happen. Is there a particular celebrity you had in mind?"

"I don't know... maybe Betty White?"

Jack erupted in laughter. "Seriously? *How* old are you?

And is she even alive?"

Dave wrote *Celebrity MC* on the whiteboard. "Okay, maybe Betty White is not realistic—and I have no idea if she is still alive. I hope she is. Loved *The Golden Girls*! Anyway, I like this a lot so let's just keep it on our wish list as a possibility."

Susie gave Jack a look that said she wasn't pleased with his remarks.

Why am I acting like an idiot?

He felt like he was competing with her—like he didn't want her to win.

They were supposed to be working as a team!

He needed to focus and try to act like an adult. He also needed to come up with something since Susie was taking over the meeting with all of her ideas.

Jack cleared his throat. "I think this year it would be a good idea to have participating restaurants and stores hand out free samples. Hopefully it's not too late for that."

"I love that idea," Susie said.

Jack blinked. "You do?"

She nodded enthusiastically. "Absolutely. Good job, Jack."

"Oh… Okay."

She's up to something.

Why was she being so nice? Well, it's not like he'd thought she was ever *mean*, did he? He really didn't know *what* to think of her other than she was an intelligent businesswoman who had opened a business next door.

But what did that have to do with anything? Well, okay, her intelligence was a turn-on.

A turn-on?

Where the hell is his mind today? He needed to focus.

His gaze drifted toward her ring finger. No wedding ring.

What's that all about? Kenneth couldn't be too happy about her not wearing her wedding ring. Maybe it had something to do with working in the kitchen.

Susie lifted her hand and inspected it, then leaned in toward Jack. "Are you looking at my hand?"

"Not at all," he lied.

He could never be a spy. He would get caught or killed on his first day on the job, for sure.

Dave wrote *Free Samples* on the whiteboard and nodded. "We are making *a lot* of progress in a short amount of time. Great job, everyone."

Why did he say *everyone*? The other five people at the table had barely looked up from their phones since the meeting had started. Jack and Susie were the ones who were doing all the talking. He glanced over at her and she met his gaze, like she was waiting for him to say something.

But that was just it—he had nothing to say. He wasn't even sure why he looked over at her. He forced a smile and quickly looked away. This woman was becoming a distraction.

Not good.

Chapter Five

The next morning Susie fastened the banner to her front window and then climbed back down from the ladder. She stepped back to admire it. "Perfect."

Her new promotion was set—an idea from Kenneth. The promo was being promoted on Facebook and Twitter. Hopefully it would attract hundreds of new people.

Susie glanced over at Jack's place and wondered how he would react to it. Men were very competitive and she didn't want to start a war with her handsome neighbor.

But she already knew Jack had an ego the size of a 747.

It didn't take long before a steady stream of customers was coming in, many curious about her promotion, others just interested in one of her tasty scones.

Kenneth gestured toward the long line. "I told you it would work."

Susie laughed. "When you're done patting yourself on the back, the next round of scones is done, so pull them out of the oven before they burn."

"Geniuses are too smart to let scones burn."

"Now."

Kenneth chuckled and went to the kitchen.

Susie turned back around and froze.

Jack stood at the front of the line, tapping his fingers on the counter.

Where did he come from? Did he cut in line?

Jack pointed to the front of the building toward the banner she had hung. "Are you serious?" He didn't look pleased. "What do you think you're doing?"

"What?" Susie said, knowing exactly what he was talking about. She glanced toward the front of the tea shop and then returned her attention back to Jack. "Is something wrong?"

Jack huffed. "You know *exactly* what's wrong. That!" He pointed to her banner again. "Coffee-flavored tea? Is this a joke?"

"No joke at all."

Jack shook his head. "Healthier than coffee. Energy boost. No caffeine crash." He'd memorized the tagline at the bottom of the banner. "I can't believe you would resort to this. You don't waste any time at all, do you?"

Susie threw up her hands in defense. "I don't know what you're talking about."

"You're intimidated by my business—admit it."

Susie laughed. "My business has nothing to do with *your* business. It may be hard for you to believe, but we didn't plan this with you in mind. Coffee-flavored tea has been around for a long time—longer than you've been alive. And it will be around long after you're dead. Which may be soon if you don't leave."

"Give me one."

Susie blinked. "Excuse me?"

"I'd like to try one."

Susie just stared at him.

He put both palms on the counter and leaned in. "One. Small. Coffee-flavored tea. To go."

Susie hesitated and then punched a few buttons on the screen. "Four dollars."

"Yikes!" He shook his head, pulling his wallet from his pocket. "Almost double the price of a *real* cup of coffee at my place." Jack dropped his credit card on the counter. "Looks like you still have a little room on the bottom of that banner. Right after *no caffeine crash* you should add *expensive as hell.*"

Susie wasn't going to take his crap.

She slid the credit card back in his direction. "Nobody's forcing you to buy it." She pointed to the line behind Jack. "There are plenty of people who want it and you're holding up the line."

He slid the credit card back in her direction. "I would *love* a cup, Susie. Can't wait to try it."

She hesitated and then took the credit card and swiped it.

Someone needed to wipe that smirk off his face.

Jack grimaced after he took a sip of Susie's coffee-flavored tea, trying his best to look disgusted with the flavor. Susie was watching him like a hawk through the window as he stood out on the sidewalk.

He took another sip, shook his head as dramatically as he could and made sure Susie could see him toss the almost-full cup of coffee-flavored tea into the trash. He tried not to glance back and count the number of people still in the line, waiting to hand over money to her.

Jack wasn't happy.

He returned to his cafe and pointed at Todd behind the counter. "Meeting in my office. Now."

Todd saluted him. "Sir. Yes, sir!"

Jack plopped down in his office chair and picked up Chimi from her dog bed on the floor. "How are you? Daddy's not doing so well. I'm in the mood to kill someone." Chimi let Jack know that life was good and gave him two good licks under the chin. "That's sweet of you and a nice distraction, but I've still got murder on my mind."

Jack swiveled around toward Todd who entered behind him.

Todd took a seat and pointed his chair in Jack's direction. He clasped his hands behind his head like he didn't have a care in the world. "What's up, Monkey Butt?"

"I need a big promotion. Not tomorrow. Today. Now."

Todd unclasped his hands and sat up in his chair. "What's going on?"

"Susie…"

"Ahhh. Not a surprise. That woman is gorgeous."

"Forget about that. She wants to play hardball. So, *we* are going to play hardball. Do you have a promo you've been holding off on? Something big?"

Todd smiled. "Promotion is my middle name—you know that."

Jack relaxed his shoulders. "It had better be good. We need something big or we'll have no chance of becoming a national chain. And if that's not going to happen *you* will work here until you're a hundred years old."

"Whoa, whoa, whoa, slow down. Enough with the crazy talk. I've got just the promo that will get some warm bodies in here ready for an amazing cup of coffee and a tasty pastry. Today is impossible, though, so let's be realistic. I need two days to make it happen, but it will be worth it."

"Fair enough. Just do it." Jack went back into the cafe and checked the daily receipts. An ear-piercing cry from outside caught his attention. A girl, maybe only three or four years old was hysterical.

Jack pushed the door open, but couldn't see the problem. "What happened?"

The woman pointed up the tree. "She lost her birthday balloon."

Jack followed the direction of the woman's finger toward the Mylar balloon that said *Happy Birthday*. It was stuck in the middle of the tree.

Jack squatted in front of the cute girl in the pink polka

dot dress. "Awww. It's your birthday? That's so cool. I love your dress. How old are you?"

The little girl pointed up at the balloon and screamed even louder.

Jack stood, wondering if he had ear damage.

He stared up at the balloon in the tree. It was pretty high up there.

Kenneth came out of Susie's tea shop and glanced up at the balloon. He stepped in front of Jack and squatted next to the girl, talking in a baby voice. "Oh, you lost your balloon? You poor little itty bitty thing. How about if I get it for you?"

The girl wiped her eyes and nodded.

Susie also came out of the tea shop, glancing at Jack before turning to Kenneth.

Kenneth gestured to the tree. "The girl lost her balloon. Not a big deal, I'll get it."

Susie glanced over at Jack again but didn't say a word. He wished he were a mind reader.

Was she wondering why he didn't offer to get the balloon for the girl? Maybe she thought he was pathetic.

Jack suddenly felt motivated, moving toward the tree. "Don't worry about it. I'll take care of it."

Kenneth grabbed Jack by the shoulder, stopping him. "Not necessary. The girl already agreed that *I* would get it for her. Let's not disappoint her even more."

"Is that right?" Jack glanced down at the girl. "I doubt she even understood what you were saying since you were talking like a baby."

Kenneth got in Jack's face. "Oh yeah?"

Jack didn't back down. "Yeah."

Kenneth broke eye contact with Jack and glanced toward the tree. Before Jack could make a move, Kenneth was at the base of the tree, pulling himself up to the first branch.

Crap.

Jack went to the other side of the tree and grabbed onto a different branch, pulling himself up.

"I don't think this is a very good idea," the woman said with a worried tone. "I don't want anyone to get hurt. I can just buy her another balloon. Really."

Kenneth ignored the woman and climbed to the second level of the tree, then the third.

The guy was a freaking monkey.

The woman was right though. They were now high up in the tree and what if one of them fell? They could break their necks!

What am I doing?

Jack glanced down at Susie and then pushed harder, catching up with Kenneth. "Just a little more…"

Kenneth laughed. "You trying to motivate yourself? Give it up."

They made it to the middle of the tree at the same time and reached out for the balloon, both getting their hands on the string.

"I got it," Jack said, pulling the balloon in his direction.

"No. *I* got it. Let go." Kenneth pulled the string. "You're going to break it."

"*You're* going to break it."

A crowd gathered below as they played tug-o-war with the string.

Kenneth yanked it even harder, the string slicing through part of Jack's skin. He winced as he lost grip of the string.

Kenneth shook the balloon in his hand and celebrated his victory. "Got it! I got it!"

He climbed back down and handed the balloon to the happy girl.

The woman and her daughter were gone by the time Jack climbed back down from the tree.

He brushed off his hands and glanced over at Susie.

She shook her head and went back inside her tea shop.

Jack had never felt more like an idiot than at that moment.

Chapter Six

Two days later, Jack was eager to return to the cafe in the evening for Todd's big promotion. He had no idea how it would turn out, but he was hoping for something big since his beautiful neighbor next door still had a steady stream of customers. Jack's sales were just okay. Far from impressive.

Jack tucked Chimi under his arm, swung the back door open to the cafe, and stopped to admire the wall-to-wall people inside.

He smiled and nodded. "Todd, you're a genius."

Todd scratched Chimi on his head as he walked by. "I know." He continued toward the DJ in the corner who played background music for the customers until it was time to begin the open mic performances.

Todd had gotten the word out to musicians, singers, and poets around the Bay Area through Meetup, local music organizations, and social media. Jack was happy to support the arts and music scene, but he needed it to pay off too. That meant the people who showed up needed to actually purchase something while they were there. He scanned the room and could see that just about everyone had some type of drink or food in their hand.

Perfect.

So far, so good. If open mic night was a success and people enjoyed the entertainment, he would make it a regular feature.

Jack set Chimi on her doggie bed in the office. "Be a good girl and you'll get a special treat when I get back. That means no barking. Got it?" He closed the door and immediately heard Chimi's bark.

"Arf, arf, arf!"

Jack opened the door. "Chimichanga, what did I tell you?"

Chimi gave him an innocent look. Her little tail did that cute wag that always melted his heart, but he knew it was just a show. She knew how to get to him. That's why she could get away with murder.

"I know you want to bark whenever I leave you, but can you at least *try* not to? Concentrate. I'm not going far and I promise I'll be back soon. Okay?"

He closed the door slowly and peeked through the crack. Chimi looked back at Jack with a peaceful look on her face. Could this be the one time she didn't bark? One more peek through the crack of the door at the silent dog, then he closed it.

"Arf, arf, arf!"

Jack gave up and slid behind the counter, saying hello to his two baristas and a cashier. He grabbed a bottle of water and waited for the performances to begin.

The DJ faded out the music and handed the microphone to Todd.

Todd smiled before speaking. "Welcome to Jack's Coffee Cafe and our very first open mic night!" He paused until the applause died down. "We only have a few local talents signed up so far, so don't be shy. Come up and put your name on the list. Okay! Let's get right into it!" Todd read from the sign-up sheet. "Up first we have Marvy Harvey, who will perform a dance interpretation with commentary."

What the hell?

This was *not* what Jack had envisioned when Todd had mentioned the idea of open mic night. Jack pictured up-and-coming poets inspiring his customers with thought-provoking words and almost-ready-for-prime-time musicians wowing the guests with their raw musical talent and singing ability.

The DJ slid a stool in Harvey's direction and gestured for him to sit.

Harvey took the microphone from Todd and grimaced, pointing to the stool. "My hellacious hemorrhoids are telling me I should stand for this, but thank you." He snapped his fingers. "Hit it, Maestro!"

The DJ started the song "I'm Too Sexy" by Right Said Fred.

The guests clapped along as Harvey grinned confidently like a rock star. He turned his back to the crowd and shook his butt, eliciting more cheers and whistles, mostly from the older women in the cafe.

Two teenagers immediately got up and walked out.

Two men who appeared to be in their mid-thirties followed the teenagers out, a look of disgust on their faces.

Harvey turned back around and gyrated his hips, wincing. "Probably not a good idea doing that. Degenerative disc and lower lumbar issues..."

"Take it off, Harvey!" yelled one eager woman.

"I'm going to try!" he said, bobbing his head to the beat of the music. "You just need to have a little patience—this was *a lot* easier sixty years ago."

"They seriously can't be enjoying this," Jack mumbled to himself, wondering how long he should wait before giving Todd the sign to pull the plug on Harvey.

"I'm too sexy for this shirt," Harvey said, carefully trying to undo the top button of his shirt with one hand while holding the microphone with the other. "So sexy it hurts. Oh, oh, oh...cramp." He opened and closed his hand a few times and then nodded. "I'm good, I'm good."

Please don't strip, Harvey. Please, God, no.

Harvey undid the second button of his shirt and struggled with the third. "I should have worn something with Velcro." He tugged a little harder on the third button and it popped free, dropping to the floor.

A screaming woman jumped out of her seat and lunged for the button. She broke into a victory dance as she held it in the air, like she'd caught a guitar pick from some famous musician in concert.

This is ridiculous.

There was no way in hell Jack was going to let Harvey strip in his cafe.

"Oh boy," yelled Harvey, after banging his leg into the stool and knocking it over. "That's gonna leave a mark. Right next to the scar from my torn meniscus surgery back in 1986. This is hard work." He picked up the stool and sat for a moment, appearing to be out of breath. Harvey's chest heaved in and out as the song continued to play. A few seconds later, he closed his eyes.

Please don't have a heart attack, Harvey.

Was he sleeping? Dying? What was he doing?

Harvey opened one eye and then the other, grinning. "I'm back and I'm still sexy!" He jumped back up and the eighty-year-old man started thrusting his hips back and forth.

Jack was going to be sick.

Harvey wiped his forehead. "It's hot in here and I'm too sexy for these pants, don't ya think?"

He cupped his ear, waiting for a response from the crowd.

"Yes!" screamed a woman, inching a little closer and pulling out some dollar bills. "You're way too sexy for those pants!"

Harvey reached for button on his pants and—

"Okay!" Todd said, tapping Harvey on the shoulder and grabbing the microphone from him "A big round of applause for Harvey!"

"I'm not done."

"Oh *yes,* you are."

A few women booed Todd and then walked over to Harvey to congratulate him on his performance.

Another five people got up and left.

Not good.

"Let's move on!" Todd pointed to his right. "Up next, please welcome Oliver!"

Oliver grabbed the microphone and turned to the audience. "So…a horse walks into a bar and the bartender says, 'Hey, why the long face?'"

A few people laughed, but two more women got up and walked out.

They were followed by an older couple. Then another person. And another.

No, no, no, no!

People were leaving and Jack wasn't happy.

Oliver cleared his throat. "Okay, then. There once was a man from Nantucket…"

"Thank you, Oliver!" Todd interrupted, grabbing the microphone from the man.

How could this happen? This was supposed to be great entertainment, so his customers would eat and drink more and tell their friends about it. Word of mouth was the best advertising in the world, but Jack was well aware that word of mouth could be positive *or* negative. What if these people started talking bad about his place with other people? It would have a huge impact on his business.

Jack gave Todd a desperate look that said *do something!*

Todd pointed to a woman sitting right in front of him.

"Next we have Felicia, who's going to sing a song. Felicia!"

Much better.

This should be good. Singers don't typically show up to open mic night if they don't know how to sing. It could be very embarrassing and most people don't want to go through that.

The applause faded as Felicia stood and took the microphone. "Thank you. Hopefully I can make it through the song without crying because I'm fresh off a horrific, gut-wrenching breakup." She crinkled her nose. "I may or may not have been a little drunk last night when I wrote this song."

Oh God. Please no.

Didn't Todd screen these people first or at least ask them what they wanted to perform before letting them sign up?

Five more people got up and left.

Felicia closed her eyes and hummed, although truthfully it sounded more like Chimi growling. A few seconds later she opened her eyes. Her bottom lip quivered, and she covered her mouth with one hand.

Then she sobbed like a big baby.

Todd moved toward Felicia to console her, and she held up her hand. "I'm okay—I've got this."

He nodded and stepped back, looking over to Jack and shrugging.

Felicia lifted the microphone to her mouth. "This song is called 'Die, Bastard, Die.'"

And it was a horrible song. Possibly the worst song ever.

Jack waited patiently for Felicia to finish singing—although calling it *singing* was being extremely generous.

By then the damage was done.

Jack's cafe was almost completely empty. The only people left were the five women flirting with Harvey over in the corner.

Kenneth stood on the sidewalk outside, looking through the window. He surveyed the empty place, then grinned and walked away.

Salt in the wound.

"Todd!" Jack pointed to his office. "Meeting. Now!"

Jack opened his office door and Chimi sprung to her feet, sprinting toward him. He scooped her up and petted her on the head. "This is not a good time, Chimi. Daddy is pissed off." Chimi reached up and kissed Jack on the cheek. "I appreciate that, but it doesn't help much."

Todd entered the office closed the door. "I know, I know…it didn't go very well."

Jack huffed. "That was a disaster. Everybody left except for Harvey's groupies!"

"Don't worry. We just need to get another promo going."

Who knew why Jack ever thought his business was recession proof or competition proof. He took his eye off the ball and now had to admit he was a little scared. They needed to come up with a new promotion, or maybe several that would help them get their mojo back.

Jack stood, walked around to the other side of the desk and leaned against the edge of it. "Please tell me you have a better idea before I get an ulcer."

Todd snapped his fingers. "Got it… Why don't we do what Peter Piper's is doing?"

"Serve pizza? That's ridicu—"

"No." Todd opened Jack's office door. "Follow me."

Jack followed Todd through the cafe and could see the place had recovered a little in the last two minutes. A few people were in line to purchase something.

Todd stopped at the front window and pointed across the street toward Peter Piper's Pizza. Someone was dressed up as a giant slice of pepperoni pizza. He wore headphones and danced as he pointed a sign toward the front door of the pizza place.

Jack sighed. "Your bright idea is to get a mascot? You can't be serious."

"Hear me out… I saw Peter a few weeks ago, and he told me his sales were up twenty percent whenever he had that silly mascot dancing on the street. The guy used to be out there part-time, but Peter just made the pizza slice full-time."

Jack scratched his chin. "Seriously?"

"Seriously."

"Sounds kind of cheesy to me."

Todd laughed. "Pun intended?"

"No. Pun *not* intended. I don't know. You really think something as simple as a mascot on the street can help us?"

"I will repeat myself…his *sales* are up twenty percent."

That was a huge jump in such a short period and could be just the thing they needed. "If we're crazy enough to do this, what kind of mascot would we have? And don't tell me a coffee cup because that would be the most boring mascot ever."

Todd thought about it. "We could get someone to dress up as Juan Valdez and stick him on a mule out front. A real mule with sacks of coffee beans hanging from the saddle."

Jack shook his head. "And who would be cleaning up all the donkey crap on the street? Bad idea. You're fired."

"You need to loosen up. Okay, how about a coffee bean?"

"A coffee bean?"

"Yeah. Remember that wedding I went to last year on Halloween? Everyone dressed up in costumes."

"You were a McDonald's hamburger."

"Everyone kept squeezing my buns, which I admit I

didn't mind, but that's another story."

Jack folded his arms. "Another story I *don't* want to hear. Get back to the coffee bean."

"Right. There was someone dressed up as a coffee bean. People thought it was a cool costume."

"And where the heck are we going to get something like that?"

Todd grinned. "I know just the place."

Chapter Seven

The next day Susie walked down Castro Street toward the chamber of commerce for the second festival planning meeting. Dave had sent her an email earlier in the day saying the last meeting had been very productive and thanked her for her contribution.

That was great to hear since she wanted to do her part to help make it a great festival this year. Hopefully this meeting would go smoother with Jack. The man needed to relax a little.

Susie entered the conference room and Dave pointed to one of the chairs. "Have a seat, Susie. We're ready to get started."

"Of course," she answered, taking a seat. Before she could pull her notebook from her bag a dog jumped on her lap, startling her.

"Chimi!" Jack said, rushing over and pulling the dog off her skirt. "I'm *so* sorry about that."

Susie smoothed out her skirt. "That's okay. I love dogs. That *is* a dog, right?" Susie giggled. "Kidding…"

The corner of Jack's mouth pulled up slightly. "Very funny."

Dave laughed. "She's a tiny thing, but sweet. She's part of the Chamber family."

Chimi tried to wiggle out of Jack's arms toward Susie.

He set her down and she ran to Susie again, licking her legs.

Jack scratched the side of his face. "She's normally jealous of other women, so this doesn't make much sense at all. It's almost as if she likes you."

Why did he look so surprised his dog was fond of her?

Susie looked up and caught Jack looking at her legs. Something about that got her pulse racing, but she played it off while Chimi continued to lick her legs.

Jack shook his head. "Maybe it's the lotion you use. Beef scented?"

Susie laughed and reached down, stroking Chimi on her back. "She probably senses I'm a dog person."

"I think you're right, Susie." Dave winked and gestured to Chimi. "Dogs are great judges of character." Dave shuffled through some papers on the table. "Any word on the live band?"

Susie tapped her pen on the conference table. "Yes! I have a lead on an eighties band who would be willing to perform for free if we tell everyone they're available for weddings and company parties."

"That's great! Shouldn't be a problem at all. We can make announcements and put their info on the festival website. And what about the master of ceremonies? Were you able to find one?"

"Not yet, but I haven't given up."

"It may be more difficult to find a master of ceremonies to work for free."

Jack held up his index finger. "Maybe you can find one who works for scones."

Dave chuckled. "Odd, but I kind of feel like being the master of ceremonies again."

"You'll have to fight me for that job," Jack said. "I'm a huge fan of Susie's scones." He winked at Susie and it almost knocked her out of her chair.

This was a rare moment and needed to be recorded.

Jack was being nice and his ego seemed to be on vacation. She couldn't tell if it was sincere or not.

Susie felt uncomfortable with the silence in the room. "Glad you like them."

"I forgot to mention," Dave said. "Tricia, our resident social media expert picked a fine time to get married, so promoting the festival on Facebook and Twitter has completely stopped. Any of you know about social media and how we can get the ball rolling on that again?"

Susie and Jack spoke at the same time. "I do."

Jack looked over at Susie. "Oh. Okay. No problem. Go for it."

"No, no," Susie, waving him off. "You know *a lot* about promotions. You should go for it."

Dave chuckled. "I have an idea…maybe you both work

on it together?"

Jack and Susie both stared at each other.

"Having both of you pitch in would give us twice the power. I mean...if you don't mind."

Dave looked back and forth between the two of them, waiting for a response.

"Uh..." Susie looked over to Jack again. She didn't want to let them down and hopefully it wouldn't be too awkward working with Jack. "I don't mind. Sure..."

Jack nodded and swallowed hard. "Of course. We'll take care of it, Dave."

"Great!" Dave said, rubbing his hands together. "This is what I'm talking about. A team effort is what really makes all the difference in the world. Okay, I'll let you two work out the details after we're done."

An hour later the meeting was over and the conference room cleared out, leaving Jack and Susie together by themselves.

Jack scratched the side of his face. "Okay then..."

Susie forced a smile. "Yeah..."

"I guess we should get to work."

Susie swiveled her chair in Jack's direction. "I'm all yours."

Jack blinked. "Pardon me?"

"Oh, sorry. I thought you were going to take the lead on this."

Jack chuckled. "I thought *you* were the one with the

plan."

She stared at him for a few seconds. "So, you've got nothing?"

"I've got something, but I didn't want to assume that I would take the lead on this."

She pulled her notebook closer. "I also didn't want to assume *I* would take the lead on this either."

Jack nodded and glanced down at her notebook. "What do you have in there? Company secrets?"

She didn't answer.

"Okay then, looks like we're at a stalemate. I guess we can just sit here and stare at each other until one of us has the balls to do something."

Susie burst in laughter. "This is ridiculous."

Jack laughed as well. "I agree."

At least it looked like he was starting to loosen up. Susie was pretty sure that was the first time she'd seen Jack smile. He had a lovely smile. He needed to do that more often. It eased the tension in her neck and relaxed her. It felt wonderful.

"Okay," Jack said, opening his briefcase. "Dave said this was a team effort, so I'm sure we'll be able to do this together. How much time do you have?"

"I'm okay...no hurry. What about you? Anything pressing you need to get to?"

Jack shook his head. "I should be fine, although I will need to grab something to eat soon before I pass out."

"How about if we order some food and make it a working dinner?"

Jack stared at her for a moment.

"Not okay? We can just work—that's fine."

"I…"

Susie shrugged. "You don't want to eat with me. That's fine, let's just—"

"Hang on," Jack said, picking up Chimi and placing her on his lap, petting her head. "I didn't exactly say that I didn't want to eat with you. It's just…you know, I don't think we got off on the right foot as neighbors."

"Jack, I don't have a problem with you. Now Kenneth, he seems to have issues with you, but I'll let you two men handle that. Do you want to eat or not? It's just food—the body needs food. Especially *my* body. Yes or no? It's not a lifelong commitment."

He stared at her again like he was completely confused, like he'd never met a woman who was so direct or so hungry. Then he finally nodded. "Yes, please."

Odd.

What was that all about? What was so difficult about deciding if he wanted to eat or not? Either you're hungry or you're not. It's not like she was asking him out on a date.

He still looked perplexed.

Oh God.

Maybe that was it.

Did he think it was a date?

Chapter Eight

Forty-five minutes later Jack sat in the conference room at the chamber of commerce eating a ham and pineapple pizza delivered from Peter Piper's. He and Susie had been working on the social media plan while Chimi slept on one of the office chairs, snoring.

Susie was a smart and organized woman and he liked that. He'd let her take the lead with her ideas about getting the word out about the festival, and they both agreed on a game plan. They both would take turns each day posting about the festival on the social media sites, rotating every four hours for maximum exposure. They'd accomplished a lot in a short amount of time.

Jack shared how he had spread the word about his open mic night and how they could target people who lived in Mountain View and the Bay Area. Of course, he left out the part about stripping Harvey and the rest of that disastrous evening.

The truth was he was enjoying Susie's company. She was so down to earth. Susie was nothing like he thought— someone trying to tear apart his business and eat him alive. Okay, maybe that wasn't fair, but when your livelihood is being affected by the actions of others, it's easy to blame people and point fingers. But one thing kept crossing his mind...

Why wasn't she wearing her wedding ring?

Susie held up her hand and inspected it. "What?"

"*What* what?"

"You were staring at my hand."

Smooth. Think of something! "Not at all. I was just thinking...and my head was pointed at your hand while I was lost in my thoughts."

She stared at him for a moment like she didn't believe him.

Women were too smart for their own good.

He hated to lie, but he thought it would be wrong to ask why she wasn't wearing her wedding ring. It was none of his business. And why would he care, anyway? It's not like he would be interested in her if she happened to be single, which she wasn't.

Yes, Susie was sweet.

And beautiful.

He had to admit they made a good team.

He chuckled at the thought of it, considering not that long ago he thought she was the enemy. He lost his smile when Susie looked up.

She pulled a small piece of ham from her slice of pizza and stuck it in her mouth, her eyes never leaving Jack's. "What's so funny?"

"Nothing."

"You're acting weird." She wiped her mouth and took a sip of her Coke. "So I should expect more random outbursts from you?"

"Yes."

She continued to stare at Jack and he finally gave in. "I must admit...you're...nice."

Crap.

That didn't come out right. Okay, maybe he shouldn't open his mouth. He was sure she would be defensive about his comment. She was a woman and she would call him on it.

"You sound surprised," she said, crossing her arms. "Did you expect me to be a bitch?"

Yes. I did.

He didn't answer for fear of a slap to the face.

Change the subject!

"God, this pizza is so good. Anyway, tell me about this tea thing."

Tea thing?

God, why was he nervous around Susie? He couldn't even speak properly around her. Maybe it would be better if they communicated through text messages.

Thankfully she ignored his lack of intelligence and answered, even having fun with what he said. "I guess I've always had *a thing* for tea, as you say. When I was a little girl, I used to have little parties in the yard with all my friends on the block. Every Saturday they'd come over and I would pretend to serve them tea." She laughed. "Sounds pathetic..."

"Not at all."

"My mom said we were too young for tea, so one time I put lemonade in the tea cups because we were all tired of drinking air. Then we got tired of drinking the lemonade."

"When were you old enough to drink tea?"

"When we went on vacation to England. We traveled to the countryside, somewhere near Stonehenge and stayed at a lovely place. Not sure if it was a bed-and-breakfast or what it was, really, but the woman who owned the place was the sweetest. During their afternoon tea, my mom asked for a glass of milk for me. The woman must have seen the disappointment on my face because she asked if I was sure I didn't want tea instead. I said yes, then I waited for my mom to tell me no. But she surprised me that day. She rubbed my back and said it would be okay."

Jack loved the smile on her face. He could tell that was a very special moment in Susie's life.

"I remember it like it was yesterday. It was something so simple, but I was old enough to drink tea."

Jack chuckled. "Most people have memories of when they were old enough to drive or old enough to drink. It's not like it was alcohol or anything. What was the big deal with your mom?"

"I don't know. Maybe she thought drinking tea was what

adults did, and she didn't want me to grow up."

Jack grabbed another slice of pizza and held it in front of his mouth, holding off on taking another bite to speak. "That's when you decided someday you'd own your own tea shop?"

"Not quite. I went through a few phases before that." Susie laughed.

"You wanted to be an astronaut?"

She wrinkled her nose like she was embarrassed to tell him. "A belly dancer."

Jack chuckled. "Interesting career choice."

"Tell me about it… We went to a Moroccan restaurant for my mom's birthday one year and that was the first time I had ever seen a belly dancer. I was fascinated by the movement, the music, the outfits, and confident looks on the women's faces as they danced. I told my mom that's what I wanted to be when I grew up and she broke the news to me that it wasn't the best career choice because they made little money."

"Back to the drawing board."

Susie nodded. "That's when I discovered something more realistic to set my sights on."

"Which was…?"

"I wanted to be Oprah Winfrey."

Jack choked on his pizza. "Seriously? Wow, you don't mess around."

"Oprah always seemed so nice on television, always

wanting to help others. I thought she was sweet, and I wanted to be like her."

"How long did that last, you wanting to be one of the most powerful women on the planet?"

"Until middle school…" She cringed. "I wrote to Oprah and told her I wanted to be like her when I grew up."

"I like that. Did she reply?"

"Actually, she did. She told me something profound, which I understood even at the ripe old age of twelve years old."

"What was that?"

"She told me there were big things in life waiting for me and although she was flattered that I wanted to be her, I needed to be myself. I needed to find my own passion and pursue it and never give up."

"And you found it."

Susie smiled. "I did. Well, after I was hair stylist, a wedding planner, and a salesperson."

"*I* was a salesperson."

"Really? What did you sell?"

"Oh…it was *so* boring. I sold software." Jack chuckled. "You?"

"I sold ad space on billboards. A *much* more boring job than yours."

"Not even…" He matched her smile. "At least you found your passion. Any other obsessions besides tea?"

She thought about it for a few seconds. "Maybe just

one…" She laughed and lit up, sharing the most beautiful smile with Jack. "We used to go to the Santa Cruz Beach Boardwalk *all* the time. I loved the Giant Dipper roller coaster and the Haunted Castle and the—" She placed her hand over her mouth. "Okay, I'll be quiet now—I sound like a little kid."

Jack chuckled. "Nothing wrong with that. It's cute…" *Really* cute. "Sounds like you're a Santa Cruz Beach Boardwalk fan for life."

"Absolutely, although I admit I haven't been there in over four years."

Jack raised an eyebrow. "It's only forty-five minutes away. Why is that?"

She was deep in thought. "I guess I was a little busy."

"For four years…"

She shrugged and took another bite of pizza, deep in thought again. "What about you? Did you have any obsessions as a kid? Coffee parties with all of your buddies?"

Jack chuckled. "Not even… I was too busy playing with Hot Wheels and Legos. In fact, they kept me so busy I didn't even pay attention to girls until I was—"

Susie leaned forward. "Until you were…?"

"Nothing. Not sure why that came out of my mouth. I think I'll stick to putting things *in* my mouth." He pointed to the pizza box. "Oh look, pizza!" He grabbed another slice and chewed, preferring to keep his mouth shut. What the hell happened there? They were talking about Legos, then all

72

of sudden he was ready to tell Susie he didn't date until he was a senior in high school. Why would he share that with her?

He had no idea.

He knew he was enjoying the evening with her. The last thing he expected was to be sharing pizza with the woman who sold tea next door. Wasn't he supposed to be mad at her? He couldn't remember why. Ahhh...actually, he had more of a problem with her husband than he did with her. That's right. Kenneth had a serious attitude problem.

Susie pulled the pizza box in her direction like she was trying to protect it. "Okay, you're not getting any more pizza until you tell me something personal."

She was playing with him—almost flirting. Jack loved that. But it also confused the hell out of him since she was married.

He shook his finger at her. "That's cruel, you know that?"

She still held on to the pizza box like she was serious. "I know. So, tell me something. Anything. I know you like coffee. And funny-looking dogs."

Jack glanced over at Chimi sleeping in the corner. "You're lucky she didn't hear that. She would tear you apart."

"I highly doubt that. You forgot when she was licking my legs?"

I will never forget that. "Okay, she likes you. Don't let it go to your head."

"You're trying to change the subject. If you don't want to talk about your past, at least tell me something about your family. Anything."

Jack grimaced. "You really don't want to hear about that."

"Yes. I do."

Jack hesitated and let out a deep breath. "Okay… I'm an only child. Both parents died…car accident."

Susie reached across the table and squeezed Jack's arm. "I'm so sorry. I shouldn't have—"

"It's okay. Really."

Susie stared at him for a second, frowning. "Okay, I feel horrible now."

Jack didn't like the sad look on her face. He preferred that beautiful smile and wanted to see it again.

He scooped up Chimi and placed her on his lap. "Tell Susie she doesn't need to feel horrible."

"Arf!"

Jack winked at Susie. "See? Listen to the dog—she's smart." Chimi reached up and kissed Jack on the mouth. Jack grimaced and wiped his lips. "How many times have I told you? *Not* on the mouth!"

Susie's smile was back—bigger and brighter than ever. It turned into a giggle.

Good.

Jack scratched Chimi on the head and then glanced over

to Susie. "I guess I can share some good news with you. Something I'm very proud of, actually."

Susie sat up. "I'd like that."

"Well, maybe I'm getting ahead of myself, but it's pretty much a done deal. In fact, everything should be finalized the Monday after the festival. As long as the sales are consistent until then…I was approached by investors to turn Jack's Coffee Cafe into a national chain. Starting off slow the first year, but then building at a good pace, and this is the part that's crazy…building hundreds of new cafes within the next five years."

Susie eyes opened wide. "Jack, that is amazing. Congratulations."

"Thanks. I hope it doesn't seem like I'm bragging."

"No. Not at all."

Jack nodded. "The truth is I can't believe it's happening. I had no plans for expanding. I was perfectly happy and content just having my one cafe."

"Oh…" She studied him for a moment. "Then why are you doing it?"

Jack thought about it for a moment. "Good question…"

Susie's phone vibrated and she pulled it from her purse. "Excuse me for just a moment."

"No problem."

Susie read a message on her phone, nodded and then stuck the phone back in her purse. "Okay, looks like that's my cue. Kenneth is having a problem with one of the ovens and we have a big corporate order of scones going out in the morning. I need to check on that before he tries to fix it himself."

"Of course." Jack pushed the pizza box toward the center of the table and stood. "How long have you been married, if you don't mind me asking?"

Susie blinked twice and slowly stood. "I'm not sure whatever gave you the idea that I was married to Kenneth. You mentioned something the other day too. For the record, I could never be married to Kenneth."

Jack grinned. "That bad, huh?"

"No. Not *bad*… I love Kenneth and he would be an amazing husband."

"Oh…"

"But he's my brother!"

Now it was time for Jack to do the staring. Once again he felt like a complete idiot in front of Susie. Her brother? How did he miss that? And how did he even *conclude* she was married to him, anyway? He couldn't remember now.

Jack thought it would be best if he changed the subject.

Again.

He pointed to the things on the table. "I can clean up if you want to head out. Sounds like you're needed."

"You sure?"

"Yeah. Of course. You've got things to do."

"Thank you." Susie pulled a business card from her purse and set it on the table, writing something on the back.

Then she handed the card to Jack. "Here's my email address if you want to run some festival ideas by me. And I wrote my cell phone number on the back."

Jack grabbed the card from the table and stuck it in his wallet. "Sounds good."

"Thanks again." Susie held his gaze and hesitated before speaking. "Good night, Jack."

"Good night."

Jack took his time cleaning up, the entire time his mind traveling a mile a minute.

Susie was kind, sweet, passionate, *and* single.

Single!

It's not like he would do something about it, would he? Like maybe ask her out on a date?

No way.

Tempting, but it was a very bad move. He didn't need distractions. He needed to focus on his business. Sales were down and he and Todd needed to do something quick if they wanted to have any chance of turning Jack's Coffee Cafe into a national chain. And even if he didn't have to focus on his business why would she go out with him?

Right.

Better to leave that alone.

Fortunately, Todd lined up the mascot for the next day and they were ready to go for another big promotion.

Jack grabbed Susie's napkin and was about to toss it in the trash, but stopped when he noticed the lipstick marks on it. He may or may not have noticed that she had the most kissable lips.

He shook his head, crumpled the napkin into a little ball and tossed it in trash.

"Don't go there," he mumbled to himself. "Do *not* go there."

Chapter Nine

The next morning Jack was up at six-thirty ready to take Chimi for her morning routine of exercise, pee, and poop—not always in that exact order. Chimi liked to stop and sniff just about every bush, tree, and plant in existence, so Jack never knew how long it would take. He tried to be patient knowing he would return to the house to drop off Chimi before going on his morning run solo. Luckily he didn't need to be at the cafe until ten, so there was no hurry.

Jack stepped out onto the front porch with Chimi and locked the door behind him. The sidewalk was wet from the early morning sprinklers from the neighbors, and that brought out a few snails.

He pointed to the sidewalk. "Careful where you're walking. I don't want to hear any crunching sounds. And don't get your paws dirty, got it?"

Chimi ignored Jack and squatted in the wet dirt for her first pee. Then on the neighbor's wet front lawn. A few feet later, she stopped to sniff a fern before deciding it was the perfect backdrop for her morning dump. Jack scooped it up, and they continued. They made it to the entrance of Shoreline Park before they stopped again. But this time Jack couldn't blame the stop on Chimi.

Susie.

She was stretching against the wooden rail near the park entrance. She wore maroon running shorts and a white tank top with maroon stripes down the side. His gaze traveled down her tone and tanned legs toward her running shoes. He recognized the brand. Expensive. The kind of running shoes competitive runners wore. She must run all the time. His gaze returned to her legs again.

Very nice.

She was listening to something in her earbuds that had her tapping the side of her hip with her hand as she stretched. Her back was to Jack as she reached for the sky with both arms, leaning to the left and then the right.

He should say something. Anything. Or maybe he could stand there all morning and admire the beautiful view.

"Arf, arf, arf!"

Or maybe not.

Susie turned around and glanced down at Chimi. Then her gaze traveled from Chimi up Jack's body to his face, where their eyes met.

She pulled the earbuds from her ears and smiled. "Good morning, neighbor."

"Good morning. What a surprise seeing you here."

"You too." She glanced at Jack's legs. "You gonna run with the little one?"

"Huh?" Jack looked down at Chimi and then back to

Susie. "Oh. No. Running is not part of her vocabulary. However she is *very* familiar with the words pee, poop, and sit."

Susie laughed and squatted in front of Chimi. "Sit."

Chimi held out her paw.

Susie laughed as she shook Chimi's paw. "Impressive." She stood back up and reached her hands overhead again to stretch and her tank top pulled up, exposing a little more skin. Jack looked away when he caught himself staring.

Susie must have sensed the awkward moment because she pulled her tank top back down to the normal and less distracting position. "I'm curious how you ended up with a Chihuahua."

Jack glanced down at Chimi and smiled before picking her up. He petted her on the head and Chimi leaned into him. She always loved being close to him.

"I read online that the two most common dogs at the shelters were pit bulls and Chihuahuas. I didn't think it was fair nobody wanted them. I visited the animal shelter with every intention of adopting one of them. Sure enough, I went down there and there were five pit bulls and seven Chihuahuas. I entered the pens and sat with every single one of them, talking with them, trying to see which one I connected with the most. They were all sweet, but Chimi was the last dog I sat with. She jumped on my lap and licked my chin the moment I sat down. That made me laugh. And the more I laughed the more she licked my chin. So that was it. I had to have her."

"Love at first lick."

They shared a laugh and then there was silence again.

Susie broke the silence and pointed toward the trail. "I'm getting ready to work off the pizza from last night."

Jack nodded, thinking she didn't have to do a thing because she had the most amazing body. "Yeah, I need to take this little princess home and go on a run of my own before I head into work."

Susie raised an eyebrow. "Oh, you run?"

"Seven days a week."

"A little lazy, are we?"

"Okay, maybe I take a day or two off depending on how I'm feeling or if I'm more in the mood to lift a spatula and flip pancakes instead of lacing up my running shoes."

She laughed. "You gotta have priorities. Well, if you ever want to join me on a run, let me know."

"Sounds great. Give me a few minutes to stick Chimi back in the house."

"Oh… Now?"

Jack loved the surprised look on her face. "Yeah. Is that okay?"

Susie smiled. "Of course!"

"Okay. Be right back."

He could feel his heart thumping in his chest as he headed toward his house. He was going to go on a run with Susie. How did that happen? And why was he nervous? It made little sense.

What also didn't make sense was he didn't think of his business while he was with Susie. Didn't think about the fiasco that was his open mic night. Didn't think about the sales being down. Didn't think about the investors who wanted to turn his cafe into a national chain.

His mind was one hundred percent on Susie.

And that scared him a little.

A few minutes later, Jack was back at the entrance of the park eager to go on a run with Susie.

What the hell?

Susie wasn't alone.

She was with Kenneth.

And he was dressed in running clothes like he was ready to join them for a run.

Jack didn't sign up for this. He thought he was just going on a run with Susie.

Just Susie.

Now he had to look at Kenneth's ugly mug? The guy had an attitude problem and the last thing Jack wanted was to go running with him. Still, Jack wasn't going to say anything. He would look like a loser if he backed out now.

"I hope you don't mind," Susie said, gesturing to Kenneth. "Kenneth mentioned he might join me this morning for my run and here he is!"

"No problem at all," Jack lied, hoping Kenneth cramped up in the first mile and had to turn back. "The more the merrier."

Susie kept up with Jack and Kenneth stride for stride as they continued their run along the Bay Trail. They passed by the protected marshland with hundreds of ducks and geese and made their way closer to the water. Occasionally, they would have to run in single file when runners or bikers were coming from the other direction. Kenneth first. Then Jack. Then her. That gave her the perfect opportunity to admire Jack's physique. The V-shape of his back leading to his firm butt, continuing down to those powerful legs that pushed her harder than she normally ran most days. The man was in excellent shape, she'd give him that.

Exercising a little harder than normal was okay with her. She took pride in her workouts and in staying in shape, but admitted it was easy to slack off when she was by herself.

Still, Kenneth and Jack were going at a good pace and the three of them were continually passing other runners. She almost suspected the two of them were competing, showing the other who was more macho.

Men were always competitive, but this was ridiculous.

Kenneth turned his head to the side. "Okay, I'm warmed up now. How about we pick up the pace a little?"

Pick up the pace? Susie knew for a fact that Kenneth never ran that fast when he was with her. This was pure testosterone talking, but hopefully Jack wasn't going to have any part of it.

"I was just about to suggest the same thing," Jack said.

Seriously? Well, they could forget about it. Susie wasn't going to be a part of their tough man competition. They were obviously ready to put their egos on display for the world to see and she would just wait it out until one or both of them made fools of themselves.

Kenneth glanced over to Susie and winked.

"I don't like that look on your face," Susie said to Kenneth. "The last time you had that look you tore your ACL and had to have surgery. You're going to hurt yourself again, I know you."

"I don't know what you're talking about," Kenneth answered. "I feel like working out a little harder today. Nothing wrong with that."

"Go ahead," Susie said, shaking her head, knowing full well what they were up to. "I'll meet you back at the entrance. Let me know if you need me to call an ambulance."

"Very funny," Kenneth said. "Let's do this." He took off without giving Jack much warning, weaving in and out of a few women pushing strollers. They headed closer to the water, almost sprinting. Susie watched as it took Jack about thirty seconds to catch up with Kenneth. They made their way around the turn and then a few seconds later she lost sight of them as they connected with the Adobe Creek Loop

Trail.

Men.

It didn't really matter what she could have said to them. They weren't going to change their mind. What was it about men and them being so competitive? Was it in their DNA or was it something they picked up along the way?

Whatever it was, she didn't like it.

Susie stopped at a bench and admired a crane along the shore before turning around and running in the opposite direction. She didn't want to think about what was happening with Jack and Kenneth. There was that old saying that *boys will be boys*. In this case, it was more like *men will be children*.

She shook her head and hoped neither of them did anything stupid. This was how people got hurt and she didn't want to have to say *I told you so*.

Chapter Ten

This is not what I had in mind when Susie invited me for a run.

Jack kept pace with Kenneth along the Adobe Creek Loop Trail, alongside Charleston Slough, closing in on Soap Pond. It felt like they were training for the Olympics.

Or maybe more like running for their lives.

Kenneth was pushing him hard, but Jack wasn't going to slow down or show any sign of weakness. Kenneth had an attitude and a chip on his shoulder, which made little sense because Jack did nothing wrong. Sure, there was that little episode of him sneaking into Susie's tea shop, breaking that expensive vase and knocking over the Buddha. But that could have happened to anyone and Jack cut them a check to pay for the vase, so they were even.

Kenneth seemed to pick up the pace even more. Jack had no intention of letting Kenneth win at this or anything, but man, could this guy run!

"I can flip around and run backwards, if that makes it easier for you to keep pace with me," Kenneth said, not appearing to even be breathing hard or breaking a sweat. "Or maybe I can just hop on one leg."

Cocky bastard.

Jack glanced out at the water to distract himself from the burn he was feeling in his legs. A man wind-surfed, keeping pace with the two of them and Jack couldn't help but think it looked like a lot more fun than what he was doing at the moment. And a lot more relaxing.

He got his focus back on the path ahead and could see traffic developing. A group of guys wearing Stanford soccer jerseys were taking up a fair amount of space on the trail. There were at least fifteen of them, so maybe the team was out there training. They were catching up with them rather quickly, but Kenneth showed no signs of slowing down. Jack wasn't a mathematician or scientist or whatever type of person calculated speed to distance ratio and all that, but he was certain it would be an impossibility to weave in and out of the group of guys at the speed they were going.

"You may want to slow down," Jack said, trying to mask his heavy breathing.

"Getting tired, Jack?"

"Not at all," Jack lied. He was tired a mile ago, actually. Now he was just dying. "Seriously, though. Someone's going to get hurt."

"If you want to slow down or stop, have at it. Nothing wrong with being a wimp. At least, that's what the wimps think."

"Fine," Jack said, slowing down, and grateful he did before his heart exploded. "Good luck with that."

"Later, Gator."

Jack slowed down and then came to a stop over by the bench that overlooked the water. He tried to catch his breath as he watched Kenneth approach the group of guys going around the turn.

He didn't break his stride and wove in and out of them like an idiot.

Jack looked ahead of the curve, maybe fifty yards in front of Kenneth, and could see bicyclists coming in the other direction.

Not good.

He ran again, not having a good feeling about it. "Kenneth! Watch out! Bikes are coming!"

It was no use. Kenneth couldn't hear him and he probably wouldn't have stopped even if he had.

Jack could only watch as Kenneth wove in and out of the last group of guys and then collided with the guy on the first bike. The impact was hard, sending Kenneth over the top of the handlebars and taking out the bike rider. The second and third bike riders braked just in time and avoided crashing.

Jack took off as fast as he could in their direction.

Kenneth was on the ground, holding his leg, whining like a baby.

The bicyclists seemed to be okay, but one stood over Kenneth as the group of Stanford soccer players made their way past the two of them.

"Are you an idiot?" asked the bicyclist, pointing back to

his bike that was now mangled. "You could have been killed and look what you did to my bike." He pulled off his helmet and slammed it on the ground. "I'm gonna kick your ass."

"Go screw yourself," said Kenneth. "You shouldn't be taking up so much space on the path."

"You were running in the middle! You're supposed to stay to the right. Everybody knows that!" The guy kicked Kenneth in the butt. "Get up. Now."

The bicyclist grabbed Kenneth by the shirt and lifted him up, swinging him around. Jack wasn't sure what the guy was trying to do, but the momentum of the swing sent them both flying toward the stinky, murky, goose-crap infested shallow part of the marshland to the side of the path. They both landed on their butts in the sludge.

The bicyclist stood up and shook the sludge off his hands. "Shit!"

Kenneth tried to get up and the bicyclist pushed him back down. He must have been hurt badly since he wasn't defending himself. Jack wasn't a big Kenneth fan, but he didn't like to see defenseless people being harmed. He didn't like to see *anyone* being harmed.

Jack entered the land of a billion goose craps and slid between Kenneth and the guy, placing his hand on the bicyclist's chest. "Hey—can't you see he's hurt? Leave him alone."

"He's hurt because he was an inconsiderate idiot. This is a recreation area, not the New York Marathon."

Jack didn't back down—he saw the pain on Kenneth's face. Maybe he needed medical attention. But first, he had to defuse the situation. "You're right. He was in the wrong and shouldn't have been running that fast with so many people around—especially on a curve. But he's hurt, and he needs to be checked out. We don't need any trouble here."

The bicyclist brushed off his leg. "This is bullshit. Way to ruin my day..." He pointed to his bike back over on the trail. "And my bike! You ruined that too." He pointed to Kenneth. "*You* are paying for it. I want your name and contact info."

"Don't worry, you'll get it," Jack said, analyzing the bicyclist. "You okay yourself?" The man had a small scrape on his shin that was showing blood, but other than that he looked okay. His bike was totaled, though, and that wasn't a cheap bike. Jack was sure of it.

"I'll be okay," the man said. "I've taken bigger spills than that. This was patty cake and hopscotch compared to the crash in 2010. Remember that one, Graham?" The other bicyclist nodded. "Yeah, that was something."

Jack sensed the guy was calming down. Good.

As the bicyclist got out of the sludge and went to inspect his bike, Jack held out his hand to Kenneth. "Can you get up?"

Kenneth thought about it for a few seconds. "Yeah." He grabbed Jack's hand and Jack carefully pulled him up. Kenneth walked around gingerly, testing his leg. He seemed to be okay, maybe just a little shaken up. It could have been a lot worse, but he'd be bruised for sure. Jack led him toward the shore, but lost his balance after a few steps, slipping in the sludge. His face slammed into Kenneth's shoulder.

"That did not feel good," Jack said, grimacing with pain.

Kenneth pointed to Jack's face. "You've got a bloody nose."

"Seriously?" Jack gently felt his nose and inspected his hand, seeing the blood. "Great."

Fortunately, it was just a little blood before it stopped.

Jack waited while Kenneth traded contact info with the guy, then the man carried his bike away on his shoulder.

"Over here…" Jack said, leading Kenneth to the bench in front of the water. They both took a seat, looking across the beautiful bay toward the Dumbarton Bridge.

So peaceful.

They sat in silence for a few minutes as Jack's nose throbbed.

Kenneth sighed. "It's tough being a guy sometimes."

Jack nodded. "Tell me about it… But we have it much better than women—there's no doubt in my mind."

"Yeah. They've got so many feminine things going on. Periods, hormones, hairdos, and pedicures."

More silence.

Jack turned to Kenneth. "You smell like shit, you know that?"

"You too."

"You've never heard of a shower?"

"I was about to ask you the same thing."

A few seconds later, the oddest thing happened between the two of them.

They shared a laugh.

In fact, they laughed hysterically.

It felt amazing.

Almost therapeutic.

Jack shook his head. "I never thought I'd be laughing with *you*."

"Likewise…"

Jack nodded. "Life's funny sometimes, don't you think?"

"Hysterical."

Jack stood and held out his hand to Kenneth again. "Come on."

Kenneth grabbed Jack's hand and pulled himself up. "Thanks."

<<<>>>

Susie was getting worried. Maybe Kenneth and Jack had killed each other by now—she wouldn't be surprised. Either that or they kept running all the way to San Francisco. Who knew, but she didn't like it.

Men and their egos.

She'd been sitting on a bench watching hundreds of people run, walk, and ride by, for who knew how long? She was tired and bored and wanted to head back, but what if something had happened to them? A man walked by a few minutes earlier with a broken bike on his shoulder and she couldn't help but think they had something to do with it. She was going to ask, but then changed her mind.

What was going on between those two, anyway? She didn't understand why they couldn't get along. Kenneth was a sweet person. A little overprotective of her, but still a good, decent human being.

Jack was a nice guy too, now that she'd gotten to know him better. She enjoyed her time with him last night and saw a different side of him that surprised her. They had had a few intimate moments too, which was wonderful. It surprised her because she had never told that tea party story to anyone.

Susie jumped up when Jack and Kenneth approached her.

Something was wrong.

Very wrong.

Kenneth was limping and *Jack* was helping him walk! They were *both* covered in mud. And Jack's face had blood on it!

They must have gotten in a fight. But why were they smiling like nothing was wrong?

Maybe she was going crazy because this made no sense.

She stood and walked toward them, inspecting her brother from head to toe. "What happened, Kenneth, are you okay?" Before he could answer she plugged her nose.

"Oh. My. God! What is that smell?"

Jack pointed to Kenneth. "Your brother shit his pants."

"Ha!" Kenneth said. "Look who's talking!"

They both laughed and bumped fists.

"Okay, wait right here," Jack said, pointing to the bench. "I'm going to run back and get my car. I can take you over to urgent care to get checked out. You can never be too safe and it looks like you really messed up your leg."

"Good call," Kenneth said. "And while we're there, you can have someone look at your nose. You know, just in case."

Jack nodded. "Sounds like a plan. I'll be right back."

Kenneth gave Jack another knuckle bump. "You're the best."

The best?

Susie stood there speechless in disbelief. They didn't look like enemies anymore. Just the opposite. They looked like they'd been buddies for years!

She shook her head, wondering what had happened.

Then she decided it was better if she didn't know.

Chapter Eleven

"Looks like someone punched you a good one," Harvey said, taking a sip of his coffee.

"I had a little accident," Jack explained, feeling his nose. "Nothing major."

He'd just returned from urgent care with Kenneth. Fortunately, neither of them had any serious issues or anything broken. They were going to be fine, maybe just a little sore for the next week or so.

Harvey studied Jack's face and pointed to it. "Looks like you got in a fight."

Jack set Chimi down on the patio next to her buddy Penzance. "Why would I get in a fight?"

Harvey thought about it. "Why does *any* man get in a fight? There are five reasons, really. Money. Power. Alcohol. Ego. Or women. Take your pick."

"You're a smart man, Harvey."

"Some guy gave me a shiner back in my day. I deserved it too, I'll tell ya that much."

Jack chuckled. "What did you do?"

"I stole his girl and married her. Heck, he didn't treat her right, so she didn't belong with him anyway. Women need to be treated right. Always."

"I agree. I take it this is Marian you're talking about?"

"Love of my life…" He sighed and reached down to pet Chimi. "If blessings were years, I had fifty of them."

He and Marian got married two months after they'd met. Harvey was a good man and Jack liked him hanging around. He occasionally would share a story about Marian, something that would put a smile on Jack's face.

Harvey lost Marian just last year. Never complained about it though. He loved to share the memories. Jack had heard many stories about Marian, but had never met her since they used to frequent a different coffee place. Harvey said he preferred to find a new place to drink coffee to preserve those memories with Marian in that other place. Just in case a *senior lady* came around looking for a handsome, half-blind eighty-year-old man with lower lumbar issues, shingles, arthritis, and constipation.

Jack hoped to have someone in his life one day who would give him those types of memories. He wasn't sure why, but his thoughts flipped over to Susie.

Well, he knew *why*. He liked her and wanted to get to know her better. Everything was different knowing Kenneth wasn't her husband or his enemy now. In fact, he and Kenneth had plans to go for another run next week once his leg was feeling better. A normal run this time. Without competition, bike crashes, and goose crap. Maybe even go shoot some pool.

As for Susie, who knew? Maybe he would ask her out.

"You're thinking of a woman, aren't you?" asked Harvey.

Jack blinked. "Nice try, Harvey."

Harvey pointed to Jack's face. "I can see it in your eyes. People told me I had a gleam like that in my eyes whenever I thought of Marian. I know a gleam when I see one."

"And I know a blind man when I see one. When's your next eye exam?"

"Coincidentally, today."

"Not a surprise. Let me know if you need help finding the restroom."

"Not funny. That's a gleam. You're gleaming!"

"And *you're* dreaming." He pointed to Chimi. "Watch her for me? I mean, if you can see her."

"Of course." Harvey patted his lap. "Come here, Churro."

"Thanks," Jack said, turning to enter the cafe.

"Life is short, you know."

Jack stopped, his hand on the open door. "I know." He continued inside and said hello to a few of the regulars before sliding behind the counter to grab some coffee.

"He graces us with his presence!" Todd said, bowing before Jack. "It's about time you—holy moly! What happened to your nose? Did you get in a fight?"

"No. I did *not* get in a fight. You ready for our meeting?"

"Yes. We've got a lot to talk about."

"We do…" Jack poured himself a cup of coffee. "Give me thirty seconds and—"

Susie passed by the window.

She slowed down and waved to him, smiling.

That was a beautiful smile. Angelic.

He waved back to Susie, his heartbeat picking up speed again.

What was it with that woman? If he didn't know any better, he would say that he liked her.

He actually liked her.

A lot.

How did that happen?

Todd came up from behind and wrapped his arm around Jack's shoulder. "Well, well, well. Looks like you have an admirer."

"What are you talking about?"

"You know exactly what I'm talking about. And you like her too. I just saw it in your eyes."

"If you mention the word gleaming I'm going to punch you in the neck."

"I would never use that word, although now that you mention it…"

Jack held up his fist.

Todd shook his head. "You're so violent. Not a surprise someone punched you in the face."

Jack pushed his way past Todd toward his office. "Come on."

Rich Amooi

They had more important things to discuss.

Todd entered his office and closed the door behind him. "Good day so far. Back to normal."

"Good," Jack said, setting his coffee down on the desk and opening his laptop. "Give me the scoop on the promotion. What's the latest with the mascot?"

"It's a done deal and we start this afternoon at three. Brian has been begging me for some extra hours so he will be donning the suit today."

"A giant coffee bean?"

"Yeah."

"God, I hope people aren't going to think this is stupid. A giant pizza slice seems to have a lot more personality and appeal than a giant coffee bean."

"I agree, but it really is just to get people's attention as they are driving by. Brand awareness is the name of the game and we should be able to grab people who realize they need a good afternoon caffeine boost."

"Yeah. As long as they don't go next door and decide they would rather have a sugar rush from a freshly baked scone."

"Well, we can't control that. Anyway, it looks like she's going to have her own mascot, so there's nothing we can do about it. We need to just focus on us."

Jack almost spit up his coffee. "What are you talking about? Susie has a mascot?"

"A giant scone."

"Seriously? How come you didn't tell me about this?"

"I was going to tell you, but you were out late last night planning the festival. Jenny from El Camino Theatrical Supply told me about the scone. She says they had to make a custom scone costume because they never had one before. Susie must have paid a lot for it, that's for sure."

"I don't care about that. What I *do* care about is the possibility of three mascots dancing on the street at the same time. It's going to look like a freaking carnival out there and that's not the reputation I'm going for." He shook his head in disgust. "God, the investors are supposed to be stopping by later. This is a nightmare. You should have told me about this."

"I tried calling you this morning, but obviously you were out getting beat up."

"Not funny."

"Look, don't worry about it. They're just mascots advertising our businesses on the street. What could go wrong?"

At exactly three in the afternoon, Jack's employee, Brian, slipped the giant coffee bean costume over his body and made his way through the cafe, out the door to the sidewalk out front. Todd met Brian outside and handed him a sign that said, "Jacks Coffee Cafe. Brewed one cup at a time."

The sign had an arrow that pointed to the cafe.

Jack watched through the glass, crossing his fingers that everything would go smoothly. The other two mascots were nowhere in sight, so they had that going for them. Maybe he was overreacting and the other mascots wouldn't even make an appearance today. Some businesses only did promotions during certain hours of the day or on the weekends.

Todd came back inside and gave Jack the thumbs up. "This should be good. Watch and learn. Or maybe I should say watch and count the money!"

Jack wished it were that easy.

The truth was businesses never knew how the public would respond to the promotion until after a lot of money was spent.

Fortunately, this wasn't an expensive promotion. Todd rented the costume for only twenty dollars a day, since it wasn't anywhere near Halloween, the official high season for the theatrical store. Then there was Brian's hourly wage, plus the cost of the sign. They could always experiment for a few days and pull the plug on it if it didn't go well.

Hopefully, it went well.

An hour later, the results started coming in and they were positive. Sales were up twenty percent since the giant coffee bean made its appearance outside. The hour after that, sales were up thirty percent.

Todd smirked. "Told you…"

Jack shook his head. "Let's not get ahead of ourselves

here—we just started. I will say I'm cautiously optimistic." Jack wanted to take that last sentence back after seeing the giant scone appear in front of his window on the sidewalk outside. In front of *his* business! Why wasn't the scone out in front of *Susie's* business where it belonged?

A few seconds later, the giant pizza slice appeared across the street.

Great.

Jack didn't have a good feeling about this and he was right. The following hour sales were down thirty percent and the scone was now dancing in front of his door.

What the hell?

Jack was just about to go tell the scone to move back where it belonged, but it looked like Brian had the same idea.

The two mascots were face-to-face chatting, but then that's when it all went wrong.

Horribly wrong.

The giant scone took a swing at the giant coffee bean, knocking him to the sidewalk. Then he jumped on top of him and began to whale on him, blow after blow after blow. He connected on more than a few punches, but Jack doubted the punches hurt since the costumes were so insulated. Still, he had to do something immediately since they were making a scene out front. Plus, what if someone got hurt? He would be liable.

Several people on the sidewalk videotaped the fight as cars stopped in the middle of the street, honking their horns.

"This can't be happening." Jack ran through the cafe and out to the sidewalk, trying to pull the scone off the coffee bean. "Get off of him." He tried to shake him loose, but couldn't get a good grip on the scone because of the material. That's when Jack felt the blow of something strong and hard against the side of his head. The force caused him to let go of the scone's legs and wobble back. He turned to see who hit him.

It was the giant pizza slice from Peter Piper's.

He'd obviously decided he wanted to get involved, even though it was none of his business.

The pizza slice pointed at Jack. "You want a piece of this?"

The coffee bean screamed. "My leg!"

Susie came out from her shop. "What is going on here? Alex, stop it now!"

The giant scone let go of the coffee bean and stood, pointing to the coffee bean. "He started it."

"I don't care," Susie said, gesturing to her tea shop. "Please go inside, now."

The scone hung his head low in shame and went inside.

Susie turned her attention to the pizza slice. "And what are you doing on our side of the street? Get out of here."

The pizza slice didn't say another word, looking both ways before crossing back over toward Peter Piper's.

Jack admired Susie's authority, but this was all her fault. He helped Brian back up and eyed his coffee bean costume.

It was dirty and torn in several places. It looked like that rental just became a purchase. That was going to cost Jack a lot of money, but right now he was more worried about Brian.

He pointed to Brian's leg. "How does it feel?"

"Not good, boss. I can't put any weight on it."

"Let's get you to urgent care."

Jack couldn't believe he was heading back to the hospital again. He should find out if they had a rewards club.

Earn points and miles toward vacations with every injury!

Susie took a few steps toward Jack. "Looks like you may have cauliflower ear and you're bleeding again. I think you need to get checked out too." She touched the side of his face to check the damage.

Jack winced. "I'm fine." He gave Susie a look to let her know he wasn't happy with what just happened. The scone should have stayed in front of her business and there wouldn't have been problems.

It was her fault.

She returned to her tea shop, not saying another word.

Chapter Twelve

Five hours later, Jack stopped by Harvey's house to pick up Chimi. Harvey was kind enough to watch the dog while Jack took Brian to the urgent care.

He knocked on the door and waited. Hopefully, it wasn't too late, but it wasn't like he could plan how long he'd be at the hospital. Who knew if Harvey was in bed by nine every night?

Jack knocked a little louder and rang the doorbell this time.

"Arf, arf, arf!"

Chimi's bark got louder and louder as she ran to Harvey's front door like she owned the place.

"Arf, arf, arf!"

Jack shook his head and waited. Penzance didn't bark at all, which wasn't a surprise. Nothing bothered that dog, not even an earthquake.

The door swung open and Chimi lunged onto the front porch, begging Jack to pick her up. "Okay, okay. Nice to see you, too. It wasn't that long ago that I saw you." Chimi licked Jack's lips. He quickly wiped his mouth and shook his head. "When will you learn?"

Chimi wagged her tail, just happy to be in his arms.

Jack looked up to Harvey. "I didn't wake you, did I?"

"Nah. You'll notice when you get older you won't need a lot of sleep."

"I thought the idea of retirement was that you could sleep in all you want as a reward for working hard all your life."

"Ha! The one thing you'll find out about retirement is that you don't have time for everything you want to do. Being retired is a full-time job."

"So why should I look forward to getting old then?"

Harvey grinned. "Senior discounts at Denny's and the movies, for starters."

Jack chuckled. "Important stuff . . ." He gestured to Chimi. "Sorry to dump her on you like that at the last moment."

Harvey reached over and petted Chimi again. "You know I don't mind watching Chorizo. Anytime."

Jack reached over, scratching Penzance on the head. "Hey, boy. Nice to see you."

"Come in…" Harvey opened the door even farther and waved Jack through. "How was everything at the hospital? Is the boy okay?"

Jack stepped inside and closed the door behind him. "Yeah, he's fine. Looks like just a slight ankle sprain. He needs to stay off it for a few days. He'll be fine."

"Good to hear."

Jack shook his head in disgust. "That was all Susie's fault. She should know better than that."

"Have you ever made a mistake in your life?"

Jack chuckled. "Plenty."

"Who hasn't? Stuff happens. No need to go throwing blame around like a dart. That Susie is a smart woman and you know she didn't do it on purpose."

Jack couldn't argue there.

"She probably already feels bad about what happened, so don't go rubbing her nose in it."

Jack chuckled again. "Okay . . . Good advice. I'll try to remember that."

Harvey picked up the remote and muted the television show he was watching—*The Simpsons.*

Jack pointed to the television. "I didn't know you watched that show."

Harvey nodded. "That Homer is a hoot, but he's someone you can learn a lot from. He fails at just about *every*thing he does in life, but keeps pressing forward. Never gives up . . ."

"Yeah . . ."

"Marian had a beehive hairdo just like Marge Simpson, except her hair wasn't blue."

Jack moved closer to the fireplace mantel where Harvey kept many pictures. He picked up a picture frame for a closer look. Marian and Harvey were posing in front of Caesar's Palace in Las Vegas. "I don't remember this picture. You like to gamble?"

"Nah. We went to Vegas for the buffets because heaven knows there wasn't enough food here locally."

Jack chuckled. 'The buffets are amazing, that's for sure."

"That picture was taken in 2005 after the Celine Dion concert."

"You a big Celine fan?"

"Celine was Marian's favorite singer. I surprised her with front row seats for her birthday. You don't want to know how much I paid for those seats, but it was worth every penny just to see the smile on her face. I did everything for Marian. Everything."

Sweet. Not all men were so open with their feelings, but Harvey never was afraid to show his emotions. There wasn't a day that went by where he wasn't mentioning Marian in a positive way. It was obvious he adored his wife.

Jack never pried too much into details about Marian's final days, but Harvey mentioned one time she died in her sleep and lived life to the fullest.

If only we all could go that way.

Jack pointed to the photo of Harvey with his children, grandchildren, and great-grandchildren. "This must have been difficult to pull off—getting everyone together in one place."

Harvey's three children lived in other states, Oregon, Washington, and Arizona. He didn't see them often, but did video calls with them on Skype just about every weekend.

Harvey picked up the picture frame and smiled. "Not as difficult as you might think. I just offered to pay for a trip to Hawaii for a family reunion. Funny how fast all their schedules freed up."

Jack chuckled and eyed another photo of Harvey and Marian together down south on the Santa Monica Pier. Big smiles on their faces, full of love.

Once again, Jack's thoughts turned to Susie.

He had no idea why. There was something about that woman that really stuck with him although he couldn't put his finger on it. Something more impressive than her beauty, which was saying a lot, because that woman was gorgeous.

Harvey chuckled. "You're gleaming again."

"Don't even start that crap. I'm leaving." He picked up Chimi. "Let's go before Harvey completely loses it."

"Too late for that . . ." Harvey laughed and glanced over at his dog. "Penzance . . . say goodbye to Quesadilla." Penzance wagged his tail but didn't move an inch. "Is that all you got?"

Harvey followed Jack back to the front door. "Deny it all you want. You've got a woman on your brain and I'm guessing it's the tea lady."

Jack stopped and turned around, studying Harvey for a moment. "How did you know that?"

"It's easy to spot love all around you once you've had a taste yourself. Like when you rent a red car while you're on vacation in Hawaii. Suddenly you notice red cars everywhere you go."

"I'm not in love."

"Not yet, but you're on *the road* to love. Soon it will happen. I've seen the way you look at her. What are you waiting for? Ask her out."

"It's not that simple."

"Nobody ever said love was simple."

"No, I mean . . . Hell, I don't know what I mean."

"Life is short."

"This is not the first time you've told me this."

Harvey placed his hand on Jack's shoulder. "You don't know if you're going to be here tomorrow or the day after. Neither do I. Ask her out."

"What if she says no?"

"There's something a thousand times more painful than her telling you no."

"What's that?"

"Regret..."

<<<>>>

Jack returned to the cafe with Chimi, his mind on what Harvey had said. He was right. Having regrets had to be one of the worst things in life. He'd heard stories of people on their deathbeds, full of regrets. The pain of it being too late to do anything about something in their past had to eat them up inside.

Jack didn't want to have regrets.

Ever.

It wasn't that he was scared to ask Susie out. He didn't have any baggage from past relationships or anything like that. It was just he had been focused on his business for so long it became a habit. But now he was having doubts about what he really wanted in life. Seeing those pictures of Harvey and Marian triggered something. He wanted more out of life. And he wanted to share it with someone. And did he really need to expand the business?

Maybe he needed to ask Susie out.

"No regrets," he mumbled to himself.

He arrived back at the cafe ready to get some work done since the paperwork had been piling up on his desk. He entered his office and placed Chimi on her bed. She got up and walked over to Jack, begging to be on his lap.

"You're very needy, you know that?" Jack picked Chimi up and placed her on his lap. "And this will make it more difficult to work, but something tells me you don't care."

Chimi lay down on his lap and closed her eyes.

Jack swiveled around toward his desk and froze.

The huge stack of paperwork on his desk, the work he had been putting off, was gone.

Everything.

The desk was neat and tidy, just the way he liked it.

"Thank you, Todd. Finally you're doing some work around here."

Jack reached over and grabbed the Post-it note off his phone.

You're welcome.

That's all the note said, and it was in Todd's handwriting.

Jack chuckled and shook his head, relieved since he was dreading going through all of that after what happened today.

What a day.

Jack glanced down at Chimi. "Well, I guess you and I don't need to be here. Let's go home." Chimi opened one eye and then closed it, obviously not believing him. "I'm serious. Let's go."

Chimi opened both her eyes this time and stood. Jack grabbed her and placed her on the floor, taking a few seconds to stretch and reach for the ceiling. All that sitting in the emergency room made him a little stiff—unless he was feeling the effects of helping Kenneth walk this morning. Kenneth was putting a lot of his weight on Jack's right shoulder as they walked, so he wouldn't be surprised if his back was out of alignment or he had pinched a nerve. He stretched again and then inhaled a deep breath and—

Jack dropped his arms and looked toward the wall that separated his cafe from Susie's tea shop. He sniffed a couple of times. He was sure he smelled scones. Was she baking at this hour?

He took in another deep breath.

That was definitely the smell of something baking. Something amazing.

"Come on, Chimi."

Jack exited through the back of the cafe and saw the light on in Susie's kitchen next door. He knocked on the back door that led to the kitchen.

No answer.

He waited and knocked again.

Nothing.

He glanced through the side window and could see Susie pulling a batch of scones from the oven.

She had earbuds connected to her phone. And…

Susie was dancing.

Jack looked down at Chimi. "I shouldn't be watching her dance, but she does it so well." He watched her spin, and then she stuck a stainless steel bowl in the industrial-sized sink.

"Arf!"

Jack glanced down at Chimi. "You're right—I shouldn't be watching." He thought about it for a moment. "Got it…" He reached for his wallet and pulled out her business card, flipping it over to her cell phone number. A few seconds later he sent her a text.

Can you chat?

He glanced inside the window and watched to see if she

would respond. A few seconds later she wiped her hands on a towel and glanced at her phone. She was definitely reading the text from Jack.

She stared at it for a while.

Wasn't she going to respond? It was a little late. Was his message inappropriate at this time? Maybe it was. She placed her phone back down on the counter and grabbed another bowl, sticking it in the sink.

He got her message loud and clear.

She didn't want to talk with him.

"Okay then," Jack said, scooping up Chimi under his arm and walking to his car. "Let's go home, girl." Another few steps and his phone vibrated. Jack stopped, pulling it from his pocket.

It was from Susie.

Finishing up a last minute order for the morning. Something important?

He thought about how he should respond. Maybe honesty was the best policy. He tapped his reply.

Just wanted to talk. I'm out back. No problem if you're busy.

A few seconds later Susie's back door opened, and she stuck her head out. "Everything okay?"

Jack turned around. "Yeah. Well…" He shrugged. "I don't know."

Chimi was trying to wiggle out of Jack's arms, so he set her on the ground and she ran to Susie. Susie bent down to pet her and Chimi licked Susie's fingers.

"You're so cute!" Susie stood and waved Jack over. "Come in. I'm finishing up for the evening."

Jack and Chimi followed Susie through the back door into the kitchen. Jack looked around as Susie washed her hands in the sink.

She dried her hands and turned around. "How are you doing?"

"I spent five hours in emergency with a giant coffee bean. How do you think I'm doing?"

"Hey, don't take it out on me. I didn't start that fight."

"Yeah, but you sent your scone to dance in front of my front door, trying to steal my customers."

"Steal your—" She huffed. "Just a minute…"

Idiot.

He should have listened to Harvey and not blamed it on her.

Susie slid on her oven gloves and pulled a tray of scones from the oven. She placed them over on the counter, removed her gloves, and approached Jack. She was a foot from him and he wondered if he was going to be slapped. Why not? She could hit the left side of his face to balance things out.

"You gonna hit me?"

"What? No! I'm not going to hit you. You've been beaten up enough today. But I don't appreciate you accusing me of trying to steal your customers. I had no idea Alex was dancing in front of your door and I'm not sure what possessed him to do so. I gave him explicit instructions to dance between the bike rack and my front door. That is nowhere near your front door."

Jack just stared at her for a moment before responding. "I'm sorry. I've got a lot going on."

"In case you haven't noticed I do too. Starting up a new business is difficult. You may recall that."

He did. It wasn't that long ago when he was in the same position as she was. Terrified. He knew he had great coffee, but what if nobody had shown up? He couldn't control people and he had to hope they would come by and keep him in business.

"Jack?"

"Yes, you've got a lot going on and I've got a lot going on. This was between my coffee bean and your scone and I shouldn't have made it personal." He let out a deep breath. "Sorry. Again."

She shook her head and removed her oven gloves. "I don't know why I'm doing this, but follow me."

Jack blinked. "Where?"

"Don't ask questions. Just follow me."

Susie disappeared from the kitchen, Chimi following

right behind her.

"I guess I should follow you," Jack mumbled to himself.

He left the kitchen and wandered through the shop toward Susie, who was standing next to the two comfy-looking chairs he had noticed that day he sneaked in and broke the vase.

She stood there tapping her feet on the floor. "You sure take your time, don't you? Take a seat. This is the most comfortable chair I have. I'll be back."

Jack just stared at the chair, not understanding what Susie was up to.

"Sit!" she said, this time much louder and demanding.

Chimi sat.

"Good girl, Chimi, but not you." Susie pointed to Jack. "You. Sit. Now."

Jack dragged his feet, still wondering what the heck Susie was up to. He slid into the chair and wiggled around, trying to get the best position. He found it and then let out a deep breath.

She was right. The chair was amazing.

Susie sighed. "You don't have to be so stubborn. I'm trying to be nice here. I'll be back. *Don't* move."

"Okay…"

Susie disappeared into the kitchen.

Jack leaned back in the chair and relaxed. The sound of the fountain was soothing, and he felt his stress and frustration of the day melting away. He closed his eyes and inhaled, letting it out.

He could hear noise in the kitchen, but didn't have a clue of what Susie was doing.

A few minutes later Susie returned with a tray. She placed the tray on the table next to him and grabbed a tea cup, handing it to him. "Here you go…"

She sat in the chair next to him, waiting.

Jack stared at the cup. "You know I don't do tea. I already tried this stuff, and it does nothing for me. Don't you remember me spitting it out in the—"

"That was just an act designed to get me mad, and it worked. It had nothing to do with the quality of my tea. You were being childish and didn't want to admit that maybe I had something good here."

"It was coffee-flavored tea. I admit it wasn't bad. But it wasn't *great*. Seriously."

She pointed to the cup in his hand. "This is a different tea. Drink it."

"You—"

"Don't speak, Jack. Not a word."

Jack opened his mouth.

She warned him with her index finger. "No."

He shook his head and slowly lifted the tea to his mouth and took a sip. He nodded and took another sip. And another. Then he stared into the cup. "What's in this?" He took another sip. "Wow."

Susie laughed. "That good, huh?"

Rich Amooi

He drained the rest of the cup in one large gulp. "Hell, yeah."

"Hey! You're supposed to sip it!"

"That's not sipping tea. It's made to be guzzled. Holy hell, no wonder you've got a line of people in here every day." He nodded. "That's the best tea I've ever tasted in my life."

"Glad you approve, but I'm not finished yet with my niceness."

"Is niceness even a word?"

She gave him a look that let him know she wasn't pleased with his behavior.

He wasn't pleased with his behavior either. She was being sweet and he should just let her. Nothing wrong with that. Maybe he was nervous.

He cleared his throat. "Of course *niceness* is a word. And if it's *not* a word, I'll be contacting someone first thing in the morning to make sure it *is* a word. Whoever takes care of that sort of thing... The Library of Congress, maybe. The people over at Scrabble. Maybe Alex Trebek..."

Susie shook her head. "Are you finished yet?"

"Yes." He pointed over at the tray. "By chance, is that scone for me?"

"Oh, so *now* you're okay with me being nice to you?"

He nodded. "Absolutely okay. Nobody does nice like you. You're the queen of nice. You're a queen in general."

"Okay." She smiled. "Better."

Jack studied Susie for a moment. "And nobody has a sweeter smile than you."

He was well aware he was staring at her lips.

There.

He did it again.

He needed to stop doing that.

Susie was a woman and would pick up on it, like a bomb-sniffing dog in the airport.

Chapter Thirteen

Susie couldn't ignore the fact that Jack had stared at her lips not once, not twice, but three times! She didn't think her "niceness" would lead to this moment they were having.

Yes, they were having a moment.

That moment when you feel something physical happening somewhere in your body and wonder what it is. Then you realize what you're feeling are emotions!

Noooooooooo!

How did that happen? Yes, Jack was a very attractive man and yes, he was kind when he wasn't acting like a stubborn, egotistical caveman. But did she really have feelings for him?

Yes. She did.

Why else would she have invited him into her place this late at night and served him like he was the king of some exotic palace? She could have just ignored his text, but she didn't.

She wanted to see him. Be near him.

She was in trouble.

"Susie?"

"Yes, Jack."

He glanced over at the scone on the tray. Maybe he was more interested in the scone than he was in her. This guy was going to drive her crazy.

She sighed and gestured to the scone. "Yes. Take it."

She didn't have to say any more.

Jack grabbed the scone from the tray and glanced at her, squeezing it. "Don't tell me this was from the batch that just came out of the oven. You have *got* to be kidding me."

"Quit squeezing it and eat it. Unless you don't want it." She pretended to reach for it and he pulled it away, breaking a piece off and sticking it in his mouth.

He moaned and broke another piece off to enjoy. "Between these scones and that magic potion you're serving your customers, you should be locked up in prison for life. This has got to be illegal."

"I'll take that as a compliment."

"You should. You're a magician in the kitchen."

She stared at him for a second, enjoying his compliment. That was the nicest thing anyone had said to her in a long time. It looked like they were having another moment. He glanced down at her legs and then raised his gaze to meet her eyes again.

She looked away.

"Susie…"

She didn't answer.

"Susie?"

She had to say something. She wasn't going to give the

guy the silent treatment just because they were attracted to each other. That's what was happening there.

Say something. Anything.

"Yes, Jack."

"Something is happening here."

He read her mind!

This wasn't the best time for a relationship.

"Jack, please. Nothing is happening here."

"That's where you're wrong."

"Look, I think you're a nice guy, but the timing is just not right for me. I've got a lot going on."

Jack blinked twice. "What are you talking about?"

Oh God.

Did she misinterpret things?

Susie stared at him for a moment. "Nothing."

"You said the timing is just not right for you, didn't you?"

She shrugged. "Did I?"

"You're not very good at lying, are you?"

She shook her head. "The worst."

Jack chuckled. "Well, don't change then. That's not something you want to be good at because then you'll take advantage of people. You don't have any intentions of taking advantage of me, do you?"

"Is this a trick question?"

"Okay, I'll start over again and get right to the point. Ready?"

Susie swallowed hard. "Okay."

"Okay, then. When I said something was happening here…that something was *me* wanting to have a second cup of tea in a row for the first time in my life. This is a milestone for me."

"Oh…I understand. Okay, I'll be right back."

To say Susie was mortified was an understatement. She didn't say another word and walked to the kitchen to prepare Jack another cup of tea.

She thought there was something between them, but she was obviously wrong.

Jack was pissed off at himself.

He had just missed the perfect opportunity to ask Susie out on a date. She said the timing wasn't right for her and he let her off the hook. She was talking about them going out, about giving it a shot. Why did he change the subject to tea after she was hesitant?

What a fool!

Maybe he was just so caught off guard by what was happening. He had no idea something would happen between them. Heck, just last week he practically hated the woman.

Sometimes life shoves a fistful of something special in your face, Jack. You need to have the balls to snatch the pebble from life's hand, grasshopper. Idiot.

He needed to grow a pair and tell Susie the truth. Tell her he was attracted to her and wanted to go out with her. Nothing less. Nothing more.

Just the truth.

And if he could enjoy tea and scones during the process, even better.

Susie returned with another cup of tea and another scone. The woman was a saint.

She gave Jack a nervous smile, but didn't speak.

"Thank you," Jack said.

"My pleasure," she replied, her energy lower now as she slid into the chair next to him again.

The truth. Do it.

"Susie," Jack began, taking a sip of the tea and moaning.

"Yeah…" she answered.

"I saw you dancing earlier."

She blinked and then looked back toward the kitchen, making the connection. "You did?"

He nodded. "I admit I enjoyed watching you, but then I felt guilty, like I was invading your privacy. That's when I texted you. Honestly, I could have watched you all night."

"Oh…" Susie said, her cheeks starting to turn some girly shade of pastel. "Thank you."

"You're welcome." Jack wasn't sure if that was the correct response, but he felt the temperature in the room go up. He wouldn't be surprised if his cheeks were starting to match the color of hers.

Silence.

Awkward silence.

Susie reached over and petted Chimi, who was sleeping on top of Jack's feet.

Jack pointed to Chimi. "She's a good girl."

"She is."

Jack slammed the entire cup of tea again. "Incredible."

"Jack, you have a problem."

He nodded and wiped his mouth. "Is there such a thing as Tea Anonymous?" He placed his empty teacup back on the tray, scooted Chimi off his feet and stood. "Your niceness is very…nice. Thank you."

Susie stood. "Are you making fun of me?"

"A little."

Ask her out. Do it now. Don't wimp out.

He moved a little closer to her. "Now I have a question for you."

"Okay…"

He loved the look on her face, a combination of innocence and fear with a touch of hope.

Jack had a good feeling about this.

He reached down and grabbed her hands, moving closer. "Susie, will you go out—"

"Arf!"

Chimi took off running across the tea shop, yelping.

Jack dropped Susie's hands and looked over his shoulder.

"Oh God, Chimi, are you okay?"

"What happened?" Susie asked, following Jack as he searched under some of the chairs.

"I think I stepped on one of her paws. I must have hurt her, all that weight on the poor little thing. Chimi? Where are you?"

"I hear her," Susie said, pointing over to one of the palm trees.

He pushed the branches to the side and picked Chimi up, inspecting her paw. "You okay, sweetie?" Chimi licked Jack on the chin and he chuckled. "I think she's okay."

"Let me see," Susie said, carefully grabbing Chimi's paw and checking it out. "Yeah, she's okay. Maybe she was just a little startled." Chimi reached up and licked Susie on the chin. "Definitely okay."

Chimi licked Susie's chin again and Susie laughed.

"She likes you," Jack said, locking eyes with Susie. "So do I. A lot."

Susie stared at Jack, not saying a word.

He couldn't take it anymore.

Jack had wanted to ask her out earlier, but funny how that thought had just flown out the window. His goals and desires changed with the flip of a switch.

He brushed the side of her cheek with his hand, taking his time to admire the angel before him.

And then he kissed her.

Chapter Fourteen

Jack had heard about people having a bounce in their step when they were happy and had even witnessed it. Finally, he could experience it for himself. Jack bounced as he prepared his morning breakfast. He bounced on his morning walk with Chimi. He even bounced as he tossed her poop bag in the garbage.

All because of the kiss.

Well, it was more than *one* kiss. The kiss wasn't planned at all, but luckily, Susie didn't mind one bit. In fact, they hung out at the tea shop another thirty minutes, almost the entire time kissing—except when Susie made Jack another cup of that out-of-this-world tea. Three cups of that tea and he could've had more.

The woman was amazing.

After his morning run, Jack showered and headed to the cafe with Chimi. He walked through the back patio and stopped to say hello to Harvey, who was already in his usual spot, enjoying a cup of coffee and reading the morning newspaper with Penzance.

"Good morning, Harvey!

"Morning, Jack. How are...?" Harvey analyzed Jack for

a moment and pointed to his feet. "You have a bounce in your step."

"I do!" Jack said, laughing. "So glad you noticed."

"I used to have a bounce in my step almost every day with Marian. Now I have bunions."

"Here you go, Chimi." Jack set Chimi down on the ground and the dog cuddled up next to Penzance, but not before licking him on the side of the face.

"So, you did it?" Harvey said, leaning closer to Jack and whispering. "You asked her out?"

"Huh? No, not that. Not yet."

"Oh…" Harvey had a look of confusion on his face. "But you saw her, right?"

"*That* I did."

"I knew it."

Jack thought it was odd he and Susie hadn't been out on a date yet, considering they had already had an intense kissing session. They had things in the wrong order, but that would change. After he got settled in and took care of a little business, he would go next door and ask her out. Based on the way she was kissing him last night, he was confident she would say yes.

"You're gleaming again."

"Okay, Harvey. You got me. I won't lie. *Now* I'm gleaming. Happy?"

"Not as happy as you."

"Well, you get a free pastry on the house. Hopefully that

will pick up your spirits."

"Funny how it does! Especially if you give me one of those whole grain numbers. The pipes are a little clogged, if you know what I mean."

"Thanks for sharing."

Jack felt so incredible he wanted to give everyone a free pastry today, but that wouldn't be a smart business decision. He still had a company to run and had investor expectations if he was going to expand his cafe into an empire to take on Starbucks.

Funny, but having a hundred or a thousand or ten thousand cafes didn't seem so important anymore. Susie had been the only thing on his mind. His feelings for her were a lot stronger than he thought. How did that happen? He must have been fighting it. That's the only reason he could come up with.

"Be good, Chimi." Jack entered the cafe and said hello to a few of the regulars. Then he sat down in his office and got to work. The festival was only three days away and he still had a long checklist of things to do, including finalizing the email blast that would go out to over twenty thousand people in the area.

Two hours later, after checking off just about everything on his list and feeling productive, he decided it was time to go next door and ask Susie out on a date. He'd mentioned he would stop by during the day to say hello, even though he would see her later in the evening for the last festival-planning meeting at the chamber of commerce.

Jack entered Susie's tea shop and smiled after seeing the long line of customers waiting to order tea and scones. Now he knew what all the hype was about. He waited at the back of the line.

As he stood there anticipating another cup of that fantastic tea and her mouthwatering scones, his thoughts traveled to Susie. She was something special, and he looked forward to taking her out and getting to know her even more. No more being jealous of her business. No more thinking she was competition.

He was happy for her.

Susie came from the kitchen with a basket of fresh scones and placed them in the glass display next to the register. She spotted Jack in the line and pointed to the side, gesturing for Jack to join her there.

Jack stepped out of the line and met her near the entrance to the kitchen. "Nice to see you again."

"You too, but what were you doing in line?"

Jack glanced back at the line, confused by the question. "I was doing what everyone else was doing…waiting for a cup of that magic potion and a delicious scone."

She smacked him on the shoulder. "You don't have to wait in line, silly. I'm not going to charge you for anything."

"Why not?"

"If I followed you back to your cafe right now because I was in the mood for a cup of coffee, would you charge me?"

"That's different."

"And why is that?"

"Because you're one of the most beautiful things I have ever set my eyes on."

Susie stared at him for a moment and then a smile grew on her face. "It's hard for me to give you a lecture when you're complimenting me like that."

"Then I guess I need to keep complimenting you because I hate lectures." He grinned. "And I don't mind paying. Really. In fact, I don't think you're charging enough."

"Ha! Weren't you the one who told me last week I was overpriced?"

"That was before I had a taste." His gaze moved to her mouth.

Of your kisses...

Susie pointed to Jack's face. "What are you thinking right now?"

Jack shrugged and gave her his best innocent look. "Not sure what you mean." He winked and moved a step closer, whispering. "Are you available tomorrow night for dinner?"

She lit up. "Are you asking me out on a date?"

"Yeah," Jack said, chuckling. "A date. You and me."

"I'd like that."

"Great. We can talk when I see you at the meeting later. Actually, we can walk to the chamber of commerce together."

"Definitely." She looked over at the long line and

grimaced. "I'd better get back to work, but hang on a second."

"Okay…"

Susie disappeared into the kitchen and returned three minutes later with a cup of tea and a scone, handing them both to Jack. She reached up and kissed Jack on the cheek. "Have a great day."

The kiss caught him off guard but was a pleasant surprise. "Thank you…uh…for the cup of tea and the scone. And for the kiss."

She smiled and mouthed *my pleasure* before disappearing into the kitchen again.

That's where Susie was wrong.

The pleasure was all his.

"Okay, let's get to work." Dave Blatt moved to the whiteboard and picked up the red pen as everyone settled into their seats in the conference room at the chamber of commerce.

Susie made her way around the conference table toward the second to last seat next to Jack, which was empty. Alex, the owner of the Greek restaurant just down the street slid into the chair just before she could get there. Jack looked up and shrugged, gesturing to the end seat across from him on the other side of the table. She smiled, nodded, and returned to the other side of the table.

Susie opened her notebook and glanced across at Jack.

He held up his notebook and then pointed to hers. "Matching."

He was right. They had the exact same notebooks— same size, same brand, even same color, white with green four-leaf clovers on the cover.

Jack pulled out a pen and clicked it a few times, raising an eyebrow before showing it to her. He looked like he was waiting to see her pen. Jack was being cute and playful.

And even better that everyone was facing the whiteboard, so they couldn't see what Jack and Susie were doing.

Susie pulled out her pen and clicked it a few times, showing it to Jack.

He grinned and nodded when he confirmed they had the same ballpoint pens. Black.

Not that big of a surprise since the pens were popular, but Jack seemed to enjoy the little game they were playing. He searched through his briefcase for something else to show her as Dave excused himself and stepped into the hallway to take a quick phone call from his mother.

Jack continued to search through the contents of his briefcase.

Susie didn't think he would find something else they both had in common, but she waited.

He finally looked at her and smiled, but didn't show her

anything.

She furled her eyebrows and whispered. "Show me."

He pulled it out slowly and showed her. It was a little white tube of lip balm.

She shook her head as she pulled her lip balm out and showed it to him. "Nice try."

Hers was pink, shaped like an Easter egg. She giggled and stuck the lip balm back in her bag.

That should have ended his little game, but it had been fun while it lasted.

Or maybe not.

Jack held up his index finger, then opened his notebook, scribbling.

What are you writing, Jack?

A few seconds later she found out when he turned the notebook in her direction so she could she see what he had written.

It's good to keep the lips hydrated...

Then he moved his hand so she could see other words he was covering.

For kissing.

Oh my God.

Dave came back in the room and Susie waved her hand

at Jack, trying to get him to hide what he had written.

"What's that, Jack?" Dave asked, pointing to his notebook.

She was going to die from embarrassment.

"Nothing," Jack said, cool as ice. "Just doodling. Everything okay with your mom?"

Jack was smooth when it came to changing the subjects.

"She's fine," Dave answered. "But my sister is on the way to the hospital to give birth to my niece."

"That's wonderful." Susie was happy for him, but was also hoping to distract Dave so he didn't ask to see Jack's "doodle."

Dave smiled. "We're all thrilled, but I have to cut this meeting short since I need to drive down to Santa Barbara. The timing is unfortunate, but I want to be there for my sister."

Family came first.

Susie understood that very well. She was even closer to her brother Kenneth ever since he had moved from North Carolina to be near her.

She stared across the table at the man who had been on her mind for the last twenty-four hours. Jack was right—she needed to get those lips hydrated because she had plans for him tomorrow on their date.

She smiled, thinking about him, his kisses, and what he had planned for the two of them. He'd said he wanted to take her out, but she wouldn't know the plan until the meeting was over.

Jack pointed to her face and raised an eyebrow. Then he opened his notebook and wrote something else.

He turned the notebook in her direction to read.

Beautiful smile.

She mouthed a *thank you* to him.

Then, once again, he moved his hand to reveal more words he had written that were covered up.

Thinking of my kisses?

Dave cleared his throat. "Doodling again, Jack?"

Jack closed his notebook and dropped it on the table. "Yup. I'm a doodler—that's what I am. Please continue."

"Don't mind if I do… As I said, I'll make this quick. Just about everything is in place and I'm confident this will be our best festival ever. We've got only three days until the festival, and I just want to make sure all the final pieces are in place and we haven't missed anything. Susie, any problems with the band?"

"We're good. They're going to do five thirty-minute sets of eighties music."

"Perfect. And the master of ceremonies?"

Susie smiled. "You're off the hook. We've got Marvy Harvey to do the honors."

"Great! He was very popular back when he was on the radio. Hopefully that will draw even more people to the festival. Amazing work, Susie."

Jack was back to scribbling again. He turned the notebook to show Susie.

He's right. You're amazing.

The man would not stop! She was enjoying the attention, so maybe that wasn't such a bad thing.

After the meeting, Jack came to Susie's side of the table and whispered. "I'm looking forward to our date tomorrow night."

"Me, too," Susie answered. "What's the plan?"

"It's a secret, but dress casually."

She raised an eyebrow. "How casual?"

"Jeans. Maybe a light jacket, just in case." Jack looked around the room and then leaned in and kissed her on the cheek. "Don't forget the lip balm."

Chapter Fifteen

Susie admired the view from the passenger side window as Jack drove the two of them to their first official date. So far, so good. He had picked her up just when he said he would, brought her a bouquet of beautiful daisies, opened the door for her, and even asked her if the temperature was okay in his car before he took off.

He was a perfect gentleman.

Jack had wanted to keep their date location a secret. Susie loved secrets, but she *loved* when the person who was keeping the secret gave hints so she could try to guess. Any hints. Just one hint!

Nope.

Jack wasn't saying a word.

She wouldn't give up. She would keep pressuring him until he caved in and gave up the info she wanted. Because right now she had no clue.

"Jack…"

He kept his focus on the road. "No."

"You're mean."

He chuckled, this time taking a quick look in her direction before getting his eyes back on the road. "Mean?

I've done nothing wrong. I told you it was a surprise, so *you* are mean for nagging me for clues."

Susie folded her arms and pretended to be mad with him. "Nagging? That's it—you're not getting any more kisses."

"What? Don't you make me pull over this car."

She burst in laughter. "Okay, that was creepy. You sounded just like my dad. Please don't do that again."

"I promise I won't because…I'm. Not. Mean."

"Ha! Could've fooled me you….you…you…meanie!" Susie couldn't keep the serious face any longer and laughed again. "This is fun." Jack took the Highway 17 exit south, and Susie was back in figure-out-where-they-were-going mode. "Are we going to Campbell? There are a lot of great places to eat there."

"You'll find out when we get there."

"Los Gatos? Also a good choice—love that small-town feel."

"No comment."

She glanced at the freeway sign that showed twenty miles until Santa Cruz.

Santa Cruz. Yes!

"We're going to Santa Cruz!" She didn't mean to scream in Jack's ear, but she couldn't help it. "Admit it, we're going to Santa Cruz."

Jack crinkled his nose. "I should have blindfolded you."

"That's it! Yay!"

Jack shook his head. "Are you proud of yourself?"

"As a matter of fact I am. We're not even close to our destination and I already figured it out."

"You're a regular Einstein. *And* you ruined my surprise. I'm turning around and taking you back home."

"Oh, don't be such a big baby."

"What's the fun of a surprise if it's not a surprise anymore?"

She leaned forward in her seat and analyzed Jack. He looked a little hurt. Was he really disappointed or was he pretending? She hoped he was faking it, but just in case she needed to say something. "You may think that guessing where we were going was a bad thing, but it's the best thing that could have happened for you *and* for me! Really…"

"Please enlighten me with your logic."

"It's simple. Now that I know where we're going, I get to *anticipate* having an amazing time with you. I'm already enjoying the place and we're not even there yet. I'm more excited than I was *before* you even picked me up. Plus, now I have all of these amazing thoughts about *you* going through my mind."

"Right…" Jack peeked over at Susie. "What kind of thoughts?"

Susie smiled. "You know, thoughts like…this guy named Jack who I'm going out with today is so romantic and kind and considerate."

"Uh-huh…go on."

She giggled. "And extremely handsome."

"You're forgiven."

She pinched him on the side. "You're so easy."

"And you're so difficult. Do you always get your way?"

"I'm a woman, what do you think?"

Jack laughed.

Thirty minutes later Jack pulled into the parking lot of the Santa Cruz Beach Boardwalk. He undid his seatbelt and held up his index finger. "Just a moment…"

What was he up to?

Jack got out of the car, circled around to the passenger side, and opened Susie's door. "Here you go…"

"Thank you." Susie got out of the car and Jack closed the door behind her, clicking the button to lock the doors and set the alarm. "Jack, you don't have to always open the door for me."

"Oh. Okay." He studied her for a moment. "You don't like it?"

"Yes, I love it, actually. But I didn't want you to think you *had* to do it."

"I *want* to do it."

"Well then, in that case, knock yourself out. I won't say another word about it."

"Good. And hopefully you won't complain about this." Jack grabbed her hand and held it tight. "I'm doing it because I want to. Because I want to be closer to you. Is that okay?"

Susie's heartbeat headed north. "Yeah…" She could only get out that one word out. She glanced down at her hand in Jack's as they crossed the street.

Jack looked over, and she looked away.

She was already a fan of Jack's kisses, but now she was having certain positive bodily reactions from something as simple as holding hands. She let out a moan before she could stop it.

Jack looked over. "What was that?"

"What?"

"I thought I heard something."

"Nothing."

Now her hands were sweating. Great. Susie was nervous. *Relax.*

They walked through the Casino Arcade and Jack stopped near Neptune's Kingdom, turning to Susie. "Are you okay? You got quiet."

"I'm a little nervous."

Jack laughed.

"It's not funny."

"Sorry. I'm not laughing at you. I'm laughing because I'm nervous too."

She let go of his hand to face him and to wipe her own hand on her back. "You look as cool as a cucumber!"

"Ha! That's all a show. I'm nervous as hell. I haven't been on a date in a gazillion years and I don't want to mess this up because I like you. A lot."

That is so sweet.

Susie grabbed his hand again and smiled. "I doubt you'll mess this up. You brought me to one of my favorite places. I have so many happy memories here and today will be another one of those memories, so don't worry." She got on her tiptoes and kissed him on the lips. "There. Feel better?"

"I'm not so sure. I may need a few more…"

She pinched him on the side of his arm. "After we go on the Giant Dipper."

"Fine."

They walked a few more steps and this time Susie pulled Jack to a stop.

Jack raised an eyebrow. "You've come to your senses and want to kiss me?"

Susie closed her eyes and inhaled. "It has something to do with my senses all right. The boardwalk has the most amazing smells. And even though many of them seem hit me at the same time, my nose is able to separate the smells and enjoy each one of them individually."

Jack blinked. "Okay, that's just weird."

"Let me enjoy this moment." She reached out and smacked him on the arm even though her eyes were still closed.

"You look sexy with your eyes closed, so please take all the time you need."

"That's better." She inhaled again. "Funnel cake. Kettle corn. Fish and chips. Garlic fries. And…cotton candy. That's what I'm getting right now." She opened her eyes and smiled. "Okay, maybe that *is* weird, but I love it!"

Jack chuckled and pointed to the ticket booth. "Over there. We need to get wristbands for unlimited rides if you plan on riding the Giant Dipper all night."

They both looked up as screams came from the historic wooden roller coaster.

Susie crinkled her nose. "I'm pretty sure that's not going to happen."

"We shall see!" Jack stepped up to the booth to buy the wristbands.

Susie used that moment to admire how well his jeans fit him from behind.

Jack turned around. "The cashier needs to—" He cocked his head to the side. "Were you checking me out?"

Susie shrugged. "Maybe…"

Jack laughed. "I'm totally okay with that. Now put your hand on the counter so the cashier can attach your wristband."

Jack felt relieved his date with Susie was going much better than expected. He felt like a wimp telling Susie he was nervous, but she didn't seem to mind his confession at all. He liked that about her. She was so down to earth and didn't sweat the small stuff. And it was true, being nervous wasn't anything out of the ordinary. Some people just hid it better than others.

Too bad he needed to make another confession.

Hopefully this confession would go over just as well as the first because he needed to say something after going on the Giant Dipper for the fifth time in a row.

He grabbed onto Susie's hand and squeezed it. "Okay, as much as I love that roller coaster and as much as I love the way you scream each time you go on it…"

"You need a break?"

"Please. My body acts differently these days than it did when I was younger."

"Yeah…" She laughed as they strolled along the boardwalk. "I was just thinking the same thing about my body." She stopped to watch the people on the Ferris wheel.

Jack glanced down at her brown leather sandals. He could see her cute little feet with toenails painted red to match her snug blouse. But nothing was more impressive than the blue jeans that showed off her figure.

Beautiful.

Susie smacked him on the arm. "Were you checking me out?"

Jack shrugged. "I think it's only fair since you were checking me out earlier."

"You make a very good argument."

"Good, because I'm pretty sure it won't be the last time. Let me change the subject and ask you what's the most you've ridden the Giant Dipper in one day?"

"Thirty-five times in a row—yes, we counted. I think I've maxed out today at five."

"I don't have a problem with that." Jack stopped and pointed up at the Sky Glider that traveled slowly across the boardwalk over everyone's head. "I think that looks more my speed now."

"That sounds good, but how about if we get something to eat first?"

He grabbed her hand again. "Sounds great."

Susie was so easy to talk to and Jack loved how easygoing she was.

Jack pulled Susie toward a photo booth. "One quick pit stop, then we eat."

Susie's eyes lit up. "I'm okay with that."

The booth automatically took four photos. They posed for a couple of cute photos where Susie leaned into Jack, cheek to cheek. He especially liked taking those. Then a couple of silly photos, which he enjoyed as well. The machine spit out the photos a minute later and Susie reached down to grab them.

She smiled and nodded her approval. Then she turned to Jack, waiting for him to say something.

What could he say? Maybe the truth.

He inspected them a little more closely. "We make a cute couple, you know that?"

"I was thinking the same thing." She squeezed Jack's

hand. "Okay, tell me your favorite amusement park food because I'm starving."

Jack looked up and down the boardwalk both ways before answering. "I'm not a picky eater, so this could take a while."

"Give me your top three picks then."

Jack nodded. "Okay, that's easy. Number one would be corn dogs. Number two—"

"Stop right there."

Jack tilted his head to the side. "Why? What happened?"

"You had me at corn dogs."

They laughed as Susie pulled Jack toward the corn dog stand. A few minutes later, with ketchup and mustard-covered corn dogs in their hands, they went down the steps to the beach.

Susie kicked off her sandals and plopped down on the sand, taking a bite of her corn dog. "Hmmm. Love these."

Jack slid off his shoes and dug his feet in the sand. "Me too."

They sat in silence and ate, both taking in their surroundings and the sound of the waves crashing in front of them. This was Heaven. Something as simple as eating corn dogs on the beach, barefoot with a beautiful woman.

How could it get any better than this?

He glanced over at Susie.

"What?" Susie asked, wiping her mouth.

"I didn't say anything."

She pointed to his face with her bare corn dog stick. "You had a look. What was that look for?"

"Describe it."

She shrugged. "How am I going to describe it? I don't know.. A look... That's all I've got."

"How do you know it's a look? Maybe it was the natural state of my face."

She pointed to his face for the second time. "There. You did it again."

Jack laughed.

He knew exactly what Susie was talking about. He had been thinking about how amazing she was and how it would be so easy to fall for a girl like her.

Like a sack of potatoes attached to an anchor.

His feelings were getting stronger with every minute he spent with her. Should he tell her something like that? He didn't want to scare her off.

"Tell me the truth," Susie said, grabbing Jack's bare corn dog stick and placing it with hers inside her napkin. "What's on your mind, Mr. Coffee Man? Spill the beans."

"Okay," Jack said, reaching across and grabbing her hand. "That was puntastic, by the way."

"Thank you."

He scooted closer to Susie, now just inches from her face. "I'll tell you what was on my mind."

"Great..."

"Ready?"

"Ready."

"You have mustard on your face."

Susie blinked. "That's it?"

"Yeah…"

"All that buildup and that's all you wanted to say?"

Jack nodded. "That's important information for you to have. You don't want to walk around the boardwalk with mustard on your face, do you?"

"No. I don't, but my intuition tells me that's not what you wanted to say."

Smart woman.

But he wasn't going to say anything else. For now.

She raised an eyebrow, obviously suspicious. Then she slowly raised the extra napkin to one side of her face, wiping it.

She looked at the napkin and then looked up at Jack. "There's nothing there."

Jack laughed and pointed to her left cheek. "The other side."

She studied him again before wiping the other side of her face and inspecting the napkin. Then she looked up at Jack again. "I don't have anything on my face, do I? If you tell me no, I'm going to kill you."

Jack helped her up. He pulled the napkins and corn dog sticks from her hands and tossed them in the trash.

"Jack…"

"Yes, Susie?"

"You didn't answer my question. Did I have mustard on my face?"

"No." He burst into laughter and took off running across the sand.

"You're dead, Jack!" Susie said, chasing after him and laughing at the same time.

He felt alive and exhilarated as he led Susie on a wild chase across the beach.

Jack had been so obsessed with his business lately he never had time for fun anymore.

This was fun.

He continued running across the sand and glanced back to see where Susie was.

Right behind him.

Damn.

He forgot she was a runner. And a good one at that.

Jack had a good excuse. At least he *thought* it was a good excuse. It wasn't easy running on the sand in long pants. Plus he was laughing so hard, which made it even more difficult. He looked behind him again and she was still right on his tail. He needed to put some distance between them. He spotted the adult coed volleyball game going on up ahead. They were in between points so he decided to run right through the middle of it. "Excuse me. Sorry. Pardon me."

He ducked underneath the net.

Too bad he didn't duck low enough.

Jack got clotheslined by the volleyball net, his feet kicking out from underneath him. He was airborne momentarily as he fell backwards, slamming to the sand on his back.

Seconds later, Susie pounced on him. She grabbed both of his hands, pushing them to the sand. "You thought you could get away from me? Ha! I was the one hundred yard dash state high school champion."

He was laughing hysterically, but in one swift motion flipped her over onto her back. Now he was on top of her, returning the favor of pressing both of her hands into the sand, careful not to hurt her. "State wrestling champion three years in a row."

Susie's chest heaved up and down and he couldn't help but notice. She was obviously out of breath too. She was sexy when she was out of breath.

"Excuse me?" said one of the male volleyball players. "We're trying to play a game here."

"Leave them alone," said one of the female players. "This is where they kiss. It always happens that way in the movies."

Jack eyed Susie's lips. "You heard them. This is where we kiss."

"Dream on."

"You know you want to."

"What an ego. No, I don't."

"Do it, Susie. Life is short."

Susie glanced at Jack's lips. "Okay, let me up."

Was she really going to kiss him?

Maybe it was a trick.

Jack analyzed her for a moment. "How do I know this isn't a trick?"

"You have to trust me."

"Don't do it, bro," the male volleyball player said. "She's setting you up big time."

The female volleyball player smacked the male player on the arm. "Be quiet. You have no idea what you're talking about. They're going to kiss. I guarantee it."

Jack liked the confidence of the woman, even though he didn't know her. He was willing to take a chance. He let go of Susie's hands and waited for the kiss.

She smiled and pushed herself up so her palms were supporting her upper body.

Jack couldn't help but lean in a little closer to her.

He wanted that kiss.

Badly.

Susie inched closer to Jack and brushed her lips gently against his, then pulled away and smiled.

She certainly knew how to torture him well.

And surprise him.

With both arms, Susie shoved Jack straight back off her and onto his back in the sand.

Again.

She jumped to her feet and stood over him. "Wrestling champion? Ha!"

Jack loved that playful, confident look on her face. He

was contemplating his next move. He could easily sweep her legs out from under her and take it another round, him back on top of her, but he ended it there.

Susie was fun and playful, he had to give her that.

"Told you, bro," said the male volleyball player. He reached down and offered a hand to Jack, who accepted it and got to his feet.

Jack brushed the sand off his pants and shirt. "Thanks."

"No problem, bro. You need to watch out for her. She's a savage."

Jack grabbed Susie's hand again and nodded. "Sorry for the interruption." He took a few steps before he was yanked to a stop by the woman who wasn't done playing yet. He was curious what she was up to. "What?"

Susie licked her lips. "This…"

Then she went in for the kill, kissing Jack with what seemed like everything she had.

He enjoyed every second as the volleyball players cheered them on.

This was it.

Heaven. Bliss. Ecstasy. Call it what you want…

How could this have happened?

He tried not to think too much. Thinking too much usually got people in trouble. Usually brought fear. He needed to let it happen.

Like Harvey said. Life is short.

After the kiss was over Jack stared at her, in awe of the

woman who was stealing his heart. "Wow." He turned to the male volleyball player and smirked. "Yeah, she's a real savage, all right." He grabbed Susie's hand again and they walked back down the beach.

No words were spoken between them, but he was sure he knew what she was thinking.

The exact same thing he was thinking.

What was happening between them and why was it happening so quickly? Why did it seem like there was a magical force pushing them together? Like this was supposed to happen.

He wasn't going to question it, fight it or deny it. He had never felt such a strong attraction toward someone in his entire life. Not just a physical attraction, but mental too.

They were connected.

There was no doubt in his mind they were falling for each other.

Hard and fast.

Chapter Sixteen

"You're bouncing again." Harvey took a sip of his coffee and nodded his approval. "That's good. I actually thought I was bouncing this morning, but then realized it was just a case of back spasms."

Jack chuckled and sat down next to Harvey on the patio behind the cafe. "She's amazing."

"Glad you got the fuzz cleared out of your brain and realized that. Hell, I was thinking of hitting on Susie myself if you weren't going to make a move. Nobody makes scones like her. She's a looker. But I should limit my intake of scones to three a day. My cholesterol is already bad enough. The doctor said they may have to remove a bunch of body parts if I keep it up."

"Right...," Jack leaned closer to Harvey and whispered. "You don't fool me. I'm on to you."

Harvey reached down to pull a sticker burr from Penzance's fur, avoiding eye contact with Jack. "Don't know what you're talking about there. Looks like my dementia is getting worse."

"There. That."

"You're speaking Chinese."

"When was the last time you had a physical exam?"

Harvey dropped the sticker burr to the ground. "Don't recall."

"Answer the question, please, or I will cut off your coffee supply indefinitely."

"You don't have to be cruel about it." Harvey shrugged. "The last time I saw a doctor? Hmm… Six months ago. Maybe six and a half."

"And what did the doctor say?"

"I don't like this game. Don't you have work to do? A business to run? Some woman to court?"

"Harvey?"

Harvey sighed and threw his palms in the air. "Fine. He said for an old goat, I'm as strong as an ox."

Jack nodded, knowing he was right about Harvey all along. "That's what I thought. What else did he say?"

Harvey still avoided eye contact with Jack. "To keep doing whatever I'm doing and he wouldn't be surprised if I lived to be a hundred or a hundred and ten."

Jack grinned. "I knew it."

Harvey had been making up all of those ailments and illnesses.

"Okay, you got me." Harvey looked up, now staring Jack in the eyes.

"But why?"

"Good question… Back in my radio days all I did was talk. Marian said I had a soothing voice."

"Still do…"

"Thank you. Anyway, when I was on the radio, I *felt* like somebody. Somebody important. Somebody people wanted to listen to. Someone people paid attention to. But when I retired, it was like my importance vanished with my job. The job was my only identity, so imagine how I felt when it was gone. I was nothing. Pathetic, but that's how my mind worked. The truth is…after Marian died I didn't feel like talking anymore. People stopped paying attention, and I got used to it."

Jack placed his hand on Harvey's shoulder. "You're always one of the bright spots of my day."

"You're not just saying that because I'm good-looking and smart as a whip?"

Jack chuckled. "Okay, you got me there."

"I had a feeling." Harvey winked and took a sip of his coffee. "I'll tell you how all of this nonsense started. One day I fell down in the driveway while I was washing my Oldsmobile. I scraped my arm up a little. It was no big deal, but it was amazing how many people mentioned the scrape and asked me if I was okay. At the post office. The grocery store. At the DMV. Out on the street on my walk with Penzance. It felt good that people cared, and I missed the human contact, the attention. I craved it and wanted more. But what was I going to do? Go around and talk about sports and weather and music with everyone, like I did on the radio? That's when I came up with the idea of giving myself

Rich Amooi

a few physical problems."

"A few?"

Harvey chuckled. "Okay, maybe a few more than a few."

"I knew something was going on because you are in amazing shape—it didn't make sense. You look better than men thirty years younger than you!"

Harvey leaned in. "I've got an elliptical machine and some other exercise equipment in the garage. Work out every day."

Jack laughed. "You're incredible."

"Are you the only one who knows I'm making up these things?"

Jack nodded. "I think so."

"Good. Let's keep it that way. My fake ailments get me extra toppings on pizza at Peter Piper's."

"I certainly don't want to mess with that." Jack winked and pointed to Chimi, who was cuddled up against Penzance. "You okay with my little girl?"

Harvey reached down and stroked Chimi along her back and stopped just before the tail to scratch her in her favorite spot. "Always a pleasure to watch Nacho." Harvey looked up and smiled. "Chimichanga."

Jack jerked his head back. "I'm not sure if I've ever heard you call her by her real name."

"I'll try not to let it happen again." Harvey winked and petted Chimi again. "Maybe we should let these two mate. They're in love—it's obvious."

Jack glanced down at Chimi and Penzance. "You want to mate a Chihuahua with a Labradoodle? Maybe it's time for your next doctor's visit, Harvey."

Jack laughed and swung the door open to the cafe.

"Jack is back, ladies and gentleman!" said Todd, a little too enthusiastically. A few of the regulars cheered. "I've got an update. Follow me."

"Okay."

Jack followed Todd into his office and shut the door behind them. He slid into his chair and powered up his laptop. "What's the latest?"

Todd slid a piece of paper across Jack's desk. "Here's what we got. We're not as bad as I originally thought. The corporate end of sales is right on target for the month, which is not that big of a surprise, is it? Of course not, since I handle it. Anyway, on the consumer side, we need to sell three hundred cups of coffee today and about the same tomorrow to hit our numbers—assuming we get our normal additional purchases of the bagels, muffins, et cetera."

"This is definitely doable."

"Barring any disasters or unforeseen circumstances, the investors will be happy with the numbers and *we* will be sitting pretty, expanding Jack's into a coffee giant empire that will bring Starbucks to their knees."

"Right…"

"Starbucks is not going to know what hit them! We're going to give them a wedgie, a wet willy, a noogie, and a couple of towel snaps on the ass. Then we'll take their lunch money and send them crying all the way back to Seattle."

He appreciated Todd's enthusiasm, but what he had just said was ridiculous. Yes, Jack had always prided himself on having a superior product and a successful business, but he didn't want his success to come at the expense of someone else. Even if that someone else was a big and well-oiled machine like Starbucks.

"Okay, I will tell you once again that I love Starbucks and they are not going anywhere."

Todd clasped his hands behind his head and put his feet on Jack's desk. "Whatever you say. As long as I get my Tesla. But that's after I buy a beach house, of course. Imagine living on the beach."

Imagine *kissing* on the beach.

Jack's thoughts took him back to last night on the beach with Susie.

What a night.

It was perfect. He wouldn't have changed anything about it.

How could he feel so close and so connected to Susie? It was like they'd known each other for years. It was so easy to talk with her about anything, really. And man, did they talk, staying on the beach long after the Boardwalk had closed. They probably would have stayed longer if it weren't that they both were shivering from the cold the fog had brought in.

He loved holding her in his arms, trying to keep her warm.

The look in her eyes after they kissed was pure—

"Jack!"

Jack jumped in his chair and sat up. "Why are you yelling at me?"

"I was yelling because *you* were off in fantasy land, far, far away. Where the hell were you?"

Jack guessed he needed to come clean with Todd. "Thinking about Susie."

Todd unclasped his hands from behind his head, removed his feet from Jack's desk and dropped them to the floor. Then he leaned forward in his chair and cocked his head to the side. "That's why you have that silly ass grin on your face."

"I think I'm falling in love."

"Sweet potato fries, this is not a surprise. Are you sure it's not lust?"

"It's not lust. I'm not like you."

"Do you want to sleep with her?"

"I'm not answering that."

"Why not? Oh, I know! Because it's lust!"

"Just because you want to sleep with someone doesn't make it lust. Husbands want to sleep with their wives. Is that lust?"

"No. That's deprivation and horniness—totally different. Answer the question. Do you want to sleep with her?"

"Yes."

"Aha!"

"But I also want to walk with her and talk with her and just *be* with her. It really doesn't matter what we're doing. I long to be with her."

Todd smirked. "You're going to be *long*, all right."

"You're ridiculous."

"I'm also jealous."

Jack blinked.

He wasn't expecting to hear that from Todd.

Todd shrugged. "You heard me…I'm jealous. I don't know…" Todd struggled to find the words. "Okay, I guess I *do* know. Look, I'm just giving you crap about lusting after her. I know you're not that kind of guy. I'm jealous because I want to meet someone too. You've never had a problem meeting women."

"What are you talking about? I don't even remember the last date I went on."

"Yeah, but I see the way women look at you. Dude, whatever you've got, give me some. Please."

Jack chuckled. "Have patience, it will come. And maybe you need to cut back on your coffee a little…" Jack chuckled. "Or a lot. You could be scaring away the women with your high energy. You're intense sometimes."

"Okay, forget about me. Tell me about Susie."

"What can I say? She's amazing in so many ways. We

had a great night last night on the beach and I'm going to see her later this evening. I'm cooking dinner for her."

"Wow. You lucky bastard."

Jack admitted he was and looked forward to preparing a special meal for Susie. He initially suggested lunch, but Susie said it would be impossible. She would be baking scones nonstop for the festival and wouldn't have even a minute free to eat.

He wanted to see her right at that moment.

But he would respect her wishes to wait until the evening. It would be very hard to get any work done with Susie constantly on his mind, but he needed to focus and try. There was nothing wrong with a little text, was there?

Jack pulled his cell phone from his pocket.

"You going to send Susie a cute little text? Put a couple of hearts at the end of the message. Chicks dig that."

Jack looked up and huffed. "You can go now."

"Ahhh, I get it. A naked selfie. Good call."

"Leave."

"Okay, okay. Man, you meet a nice girl and suddenly you forget who your friends are. Not cool."

Jack waited for Todd to close the door behind him. Then he texted Susie.

Looking forward to spoiling you this evening for dinner. I hope you'll be hungry.

He added a heart at the end and pressed send. A couple of minutes later Susie replied.

I'm already hungry now, so imagine how starving I'll be when I see you. I'm going to wrestle you for the food.

Jack smiled and replied.

You won't have a chance, but I look forward to your trying.

Susie smiled and set the phone back down on the counter. Time to get back to work. Just the thought of wrestling with Jack made her giddy. She loved that he was thinking of her already since it was only nine in the morning. The truth was she had been thinking about him too. Even had had a dream about him.

"There's that smile again," Kenneth said, entering the kitchen with an empty basket. He reached for some scones to fill the basket.

"Don't touch those—they're for tomorrow." Susie pointed to the rack of scones behind her. "Over there."

"Okay." Kenneth passed behind Susie to fill his basket with scones. "You seeing him again tonight?"

Susie nodded and slipped the oven gloves back on. "Yeah…" She opened the top oven door and pulled out another rack of freshly baked scones. She slid them on the counter and took off the gloves. "He's cooking dinner for me at his place."

Susie had already filled Kenneth in on their date last night at the Santa Cruz Beach Boardwalk. He questioned her strong feelings for Jack, bringing up the fact that they'd just met. She assured him they were real and strong feelings and that sometimes you know when you have a good thing staring you in the face. And grabbing your hand. And hugging you when you're cold.

She especially loved that part.

Kenneth filled his basket with more scones and pushed the kitchen door open to head back to the front counter. Then he paused and looked back. "Tell him I would be okay if he made dinner for me too. I have no problem being a third wheel."

Susie laughed and grabbed the next tray of scones ready to go in the oven. It would be a crazy day preparing for the festival. She'd gotten there at four in the morning to prepare the scones and even with one of her employees helping her it was a lot of work.

Thank God Kenneth managed the shop.

She estimated she would finish around six in the evening. Fourteen hours of baking, but she wouldn't complain one bit.

This wouldn't be something she had to do every day, and

she wanted to be the hit of the festival with her scones. This would put her on the map. Everything was going according to plan, and she looked forward to having a business that had regulars, just like Jack's cafe.

She caught herself smiling again at the thought of Jack.

How lucky was she?

A new business and a new man in the same week!

Susie was on cloud nine, but it was time to dig in and keep going.

"Five hours down, nine to go," she mumbled to herself.

Exactly eight and a half hours later, Susie removed her apron and leaned against the counter. It felt good to finish up before five, a half hour earlier than she had thought she would. She surveyed the disaster that was her kitchen. She didn't think it could be so messy. There was flour, sugar, and dough on just about every surface. But she did it. She eyed the racks and racks of scones and felt pride surging through her system. Grandma would be proud.

Susie washed her hands in the sink and grabbed the towel to dry them. She was done. She was pooped. She was excited to see Jack.

She just needed to drop by the house for a quick shower to freshen up, and hopefully that would give her a much-needed boost of energy. Then it would be dinner at seven with the man that had been on her mind all day. She had already warned him it wouldn't be a long night because she needed to get up early in the morning. But spending any time with Jack was a good thing. They had a strong connection, and she had a good feeling about him.

The kitchen door swung open, startling Susie. It was her employee, Alex. He limped in, still a little sore from his fight with the coffee bean. All the other employees had left for the day, including Kenneth who went to make a Costco run to pick up a few things for the festival tomorrow. Alex had been begging for more hours, so Susie found a few more things for him to do even though she was still disappointed with him for his behavior the other day.

Susie moved one of the baking racks closer to the wall. "All done?"

"Yeah…" Alex pointed back toward the other side of the kitchen door. "Some guy wants to talk to you outside."

"Okay, thanks." Susie pushed open the kitchen door, walked past the register. A large man in a navy blue suit stood there, staring down at his clipboard. He was bald, around fifty years old. He had a badge on the chest of his jacket and a patch of some type on his arm. He looked official. "Hi. Can I help you?"

The man looked up from his clipboard. "Are you the proprietor, Susie McKenna?"

"Yes."

He pulled a piece of paper from his clipboard and handed it to her. "I'm the Fire Marshal."

Susie stared at the three words at the top of the official-looking document from the city of Mountain View.

Rich Amooi

Cease and Desist.

She squished her eyebrows together and swallowed hard. "I'm not sure I understand."

She didn't like the serious look on the man's face.

He cleared his throat and pointed to the document in her hands. "It's an official notice about your multiple code violations. I'm shutting your business down."

Chapter Seventeen

Jack was worried. Susie was supposed to arrive over an hour ago and was still a no-show. He'd already sent her two text messages to get an update on when she would be there and even had left a voicemail message. Not even one response from her.

He knew she would have a crazy day baking, but she'd replied to many of his earlier text messages. They agreed she would come to his house around seven, but eight o'clock was not considered "around seven." Maybe she went home to shower and fell asleep on the bed—definitely a possibility since she had worked sixteen hours today.

It was the uncertainty that was killing Jack. He didn't think she had changed her mind about the two of them, so what could it be? Hopefully, she was okay.

He opened the oven to check on the chicken enchiladas, Susie's favorite dish, which would be a surprise. They still looked moist. Good thing he turned off the oven and covered the casserole dish with aluminum foil a long time ago.

"What should I do?" Jack asked Chimi, who was still sticking close by in case Jack dropped another piece of cheese on the floor.

Chimi just stared up at Jack and then looked over toward the stove. "Arf!"

"Right. You're not getting any of that. The cheese is okay, but you know you can't eat chicken." He glanced over at the unopened bottle of his favorite Noble Vines 337 Cabernet. Maybe a glass would take the edge off. "I guess there's no harm in opening that now. Looks like your dad may be drinking alone tonight."

Chimi gave him a sympathetic look. Or maybe the dog was just confused. Jack opened the bottle and poured himself a glass. Then he got comfortable in the dining room. He took a sip of wine and double-checked his phone to see if he had missed a message that had come in.

Nothing.

He sighed and took another sip of his wine, then lifted Chimi to his lap. "I had high expectations for tonight, Chimi. It felt so good to cook for someone else, you know?"

Chimi licked Jack on the hand.

"No. You don't know. You're just a funny-looking dog who likes to cuddle." Jack took another sip of wine, then Chimi licked him on the neck. "Okay, maybe I feel a little guilty saying that. I'm lucky I found you, you know that? You may think that I rescued you, but I think you rescued me. It's good to have you around." Jack kissed Chimi on the head. "I'm glad we had this conversation."

Chimi reached up and kissed Jack on the lips.

"How many times have I told you? *Not* on the mouth. That's disgusting."

The doorbell rang.

"Arf, arf, arf!"

Chimi leaped from Jack's lap and sprinted toward the front door. Jack placed his glass of wine on the kitchen counter, happy to know Susie was finally there.

His heart rate shot through the roof just thinking of her. He promised himself he wouldn't make a big deal of her being so late. Wouldn't even mention it. She had a long day and he would patiently listen and just appreciate the fact that he could still enjoy her company.

Jack opened the front door and got a big surprise.

It was Kenneth, and he didn't look happy.

"What happened?" Jack asked, now worried that something was wrong with Susie. "Is Susie okay?"

"No, she's *not* okay." Kenneth grabbed Jack by the shirt and pulled him out of the house, dragging him across the porch to the front lawn.

Jack tried to break free from his grip. "Hey! What are you doing? Let go of me!"

"Arf, arf, arf!"

Kenneth swung Jack around so he was facing him and let loose a strong jab that connected with Jack's jaw. It was so fast Jack barely saw it coming. His fall to the ground was just as fast.

"Grrrrrrrrrr." Chimi grabbed a hold of the bottom of

Kenneth's pant leg and yanked it back and forth, trying to tear it apart. Jack had never heard her growl like that, but she was trying to protect him.

Jack was on his back on the lawn looking up at Kenneth. His jaw vibrated with pain. His mind filled with confusion. This didn't make any sense. They were friends now!

"You bastard!" Kenneth yelled. "Get up so I can knock you back down again."

Jack rolled over to his side and pushed himself back up onto his feet. He felt his jaw with his hand, then opened and closed his mouth a few times.

Kenneth pushed Jack in the chest. "How could you do such a thing?"

"What did I do? What are you talking about?"

Kenneth jabbed him in the chest with a finger "You know *exactly* what you did. Don't play stupid with me!"

Jack held his hands in the air. "Stop for a moment, would you? Tell me what I did and *why* you're acting this way."

"Arf, arf, arf!"

"Chimi, enough." Jack picked up Chimi and tucked her under his arm.

Kenneth pulled a folded piece of paper from his back pocket and handed it to Jack. "You did this. You threatened to report us and you did. Don't even try to deny it."

Jack unfolded the piece of paper, still feeling the pain in his jaw. He read the document from the city of Mountain

View. It was a cease and desist order for Susie's Tea and Scones.

Jack stared at it again, trying to piece together what had happened. "Oh God."

This was a nightmare.

The festival was tomorrow.

Kenneth yanked the document back out of Jack's hands. "How could you do this? I thought you and my sister had something going on." Kenneth gave Jack a look of disgust. "You played us for fools, pretended to like us, while all along you were just waiting for the fire marshal to come around and shut us down."

"I think you're overlooking the fact that *you* had serious problems and didn't fix them!"

"I was going to fix them. I had the parts on order! But *you* ratted us out like a spoiled little kid!"

Jack's worst nightmare was unfolding right before his eyes. Susie's business was shut down right before the biggest day of the year. He would also lose *her* over this. He wouldn't blame her one bit for thinking he was the most despicable person on the planet because he was.

He ran his fingers through his hair, trying to think.

Kenneth paced back and forth. "We've sunk over two hundred thousand dollars into that business to get it up and running. This little stunt of yours could ruin us. Do you get that?"

Jack nodded. "Yes. Completely. But you have to believe

me when I tell you I *never* mailed the complaint. Yes, I filled out the form, but I left it on my desk. One of my employees must have mailed it. I swear. I'm going to fix this."

Kenneth studied Jack for a moment. "How exactly are you going to do that?"

"I don't know, but I will. You have to believe me."

"I don't know what we're going to do. We can't open the tea shop again until all the code violations are corrected and inspected by the fire marshal. He doesn't work on the weekends, which means there is *no way* we can be open for the festival tomorrow. We're screwed unless there is another way around this that my mind can't come up with at the moment."

Jack nodded, deep in thought. "Was Susie able to finish baking all the scones?"

"Yes. What does that have to do with anything?"

"Come inside."

Kenneth glanced toward the open front door. "Why would I want to go inside your house?"

Jack stopped and turned around. "I'm going to fix this— I promise. But I'll need your help."

Kenneth was hesitant, but then followed Jack inside to the kitchen.

"Let me get you a drink." Jack grabbed the bottle of wine.

Kenneth waved off the bottle. "That's not strong enough for how I'm feeling right now. I need something closer to paint thinner."

Jack walked over to the pantry and came out with a bottle of tequila, holding it up. "Better?"

"Much." Kenneth drained his shot of tequila and held the shot glass out for a refill. Jack filled the glass and Kenneth drank that one as well.

Then Jack picked up his glass of wine from the counter and drank all of it in one gulp. "Okay. First, how's Susie?"

"How do you *think* she is?"

Jack nodded. "Dumb question. She's pissed off."

"No. *I'm* pissed off. She's much worse. She's heartbroken. Devastated. You betrayed her."

"That's why she hasn't returned my text messages or calls." He ran his fingers through his hair. "Where is she?"

"She won't tell me, but she's a big girl. Susie's the most resilient person I know and can bounce back from just about anything. But I know my sister and she's not going to talk to you ever again if you don't fix this, so you better come up with a plan. Forget about her for the moment."

Forget about her for a moment?

Impossible.

Jack wasn't going to forget about her ever. Especially if he lost her.

He pulled out his cell phone. "We need backup."

An hour later, Jack was back at his cafe with Kenneth, Todd, and Harvey. Chimi and Penzance cuddled in the corner as the guys brainstormed on how to get him out of that big, fat mess he had created.

Jack read the cease and desist order for the fourth time, trying to see if there was any way around it. "Okay, it specifies that Susie and Kenneth cannot operate their business out of their building. If they do, they could be shut down permanently, be fined, and face possible jail time. But it doesn't specify anywhere here that they can't operate the business out of *another* building."

Kenneth took the document back from Jack and inspected it. "What are you suggesting? We pick up our business and move in the middle of the night?"

"Basically."

He was sure they had a plan that would work, but it meant working through the night.

No sleep for the weary.

Kenneth huffed. "Do you know how long it took us to move all of that stuff in there? And you expect us to move everything in the next twelve hours? And where would we go, even if we were able to pull it off?"

Jack took a step toward Kenneth and gestured around his cafe. "Right here."

"What?" Todd asked, finally saying something. "This is ridiculous *and* impossible."

Jack shook his head. "I don't think it is. We're not going

to move everything. We'll move our tables and chairs out of the building to the back parking lot. Then we'll move Susie's stuff in. Not everything. Just the furniture, some plants, a fountain or two, and of course the teapots and scones."

The plan seemed feasible, but it wouldn't be easy. They would have to work as a team to make it happen. Susie wouldn't have a clue what was going on since she hadn't returned Jack's calls, but he wasn't going to worry about that now. He needed to fix this and he would do whatever it took. Even if it meant sacrificing his own business and his own future.

He didn't want to lose Susie over this.

He couldn't.

"Count me in," Harvey said, enthusiastically. "You can pay me in scones—that's all I ask. And since I'll be the master of ceremonies for the festival, I can give extra mentions on the microphone to Susie's business and announce they'll have some specials or a celebration when they reopen. Whatever you want me to say."

Jack squeezed Harvey's shoulder. "*Great* idea! We need to get as many flyers in the hands of festival guests as possible. Todd can use his graphic design magic to come up with something brilliant and we'll have them printed at the copy place the moment they open in the—"

Todd held up his index finger. "Can I talk to you for a moment?"

"Uh… Okay." Jack gestured to his office. "We'll be right

back, guys."

Todd followed Jack into his office and closed the door.

Jack leaned against his desk. "I know it's late and I know I'm asking a lot of you. I'll throw in a bonus in your next paycheck for your extra time, okay?"

"How much of a bonus? Enough to pay for a Tesla and a beach house?"

Jack blinked twice. "Oh. Okay, I get it now."

He had promised Todd he would be made a partner if the deal went through with the investors. That meant a huge raise for him, plus stock if the company ever went public.

Todd pressed his palms to his temples. "You're crazy. We won't hit our sales goals with your plan. That means the investors will bail on us and the possibility of having a chain of cafes around the country would disappear. Is that what you want?"

"I want Susie."

Jack wouldn't get mad at Todd because he wanted the company to expand. Yes, Todd was focused on the money, but Jack didn't care about the money and it was his company. The truth was he'd lost a little of his focus and passion when the investors came into the mix.

Not anymore.

Todd shook his head. "You really messed things up and *I'm* going to pay the price for it."

"Hey, technically *you* messed up. You're the one who mailed that letter."

"I was just trying to help."

"I know, I know. That's the past and we can't change that. The only thing we can do now is try to repair the damage. Most new restaurants and businesses end up closing within the first year. It's not easy and I don't want to be the cause of Susie's business disappearing. And more importantly, I don't want *Susie* to disappear from my life, which is what will happen if we don't fix this."

Todd frowned but didn't respond.

"Look, before this idea of expansion came along you were *very* happy working here. I think I've been more than generous with your salary *and* flexible with your time off."

Todd sighed. "And I appreciate it very much, but I got caught up in the thought of all that money coming our way. It was *a lot* of money."

Jack couldn't argue with Todd about that point. It *was* a lot. "Look what happened to John. Money doesn't guarantee happiness."

John was a guy they went to high school with. He invented a new software program and made a fortune. Since then he got divorced and turned to drugs.

That didn't sound like a person who was happy.

Jack squeezed Todd's shoulder. "Who knows what's waiting for us in the future—another opportunity can come our way. You'll probably still get that Tesla and the beach house, if that's what you really want. Anything is possible, right?"

"Right…"

"So? Can I count on you?"

Todd hesitated and then shrugged. "Yeah…" Todd gave Jack a hug. "Of course."

Jack slapped Todd on the back. "Good. Come on."

They joined Kenneth and Harvey out in the cafe and Jack pointed to the food. "Eat some food, guys. You'll need the strength if we're going to pull an all-nighter." Jack handed Harvey a plate of the chicken enchiladas he had made for Susie.

"Thank you," Harvey said, digging in. "These late night dinners are not the best for my heartburn or digestive tract issues, but I'm willing to suffer a little for the cause."

Jack winked at Harvey. "You're a good man."

Chapter Eighteen

The next morning Susie left the house early and drove over the hill to Santa Cruz. She had barely slept at all and wanted to make an escape to clear her head. Being by the ocean always seemed to help. The plan was to go for a walk on the beach and then ride the Giant Dipper over and over again until she forgot about her problems or got sick.

Last night wasn't a good night.

Especially with the text messages and calls from Jack. The truth was she just didn't feel like talking to anybody. Especially him.

Jack had betrayed her.

Yes, Kenneth should have fixed those problems, but why didn't Jack come to her? Because he didn't care, that's why. She still couldn't believe what he had done and how he had pretended to like her. What kind of sick game was that guy playing? She had never met a man so cruel, toying with her emotions like that. All just so he could have her shut down right before the festival. It was wrong on so many levels.

The worst part was her hands were tied. There was nothing she could do about her tea shop being shut down until Monday. The festival would be long over by then, along with possibly any hope of having a successful business in downtown Mountain View.

Kenneth had returned to the tea shop yesterday after the fire marshal had shut them down. He had been furious and said he was going to pay Jack a visit and introduce his fist to Jack's face. Susie told Kenneth violence wouldn't solve anything, but of course her brother hadn't listened because he was a stubborn man. Susie ended up turning her phone off after that because she didn't want to know what happened and certainly didn't want to get any calls from Jack trying to justify his actions.

There was no excuse.

The atmosphere at the beach was much different this time than when she was there with Jack. It was still early, and the boardwalk hadn't opened yet. The only sound came from the seagulls, a few distant seals barking, and the crashing of the waves. There weren't many people on the beach at all. Susie counted three people out for a morning walk on the sand. There was a woman doing yoga by the volleyball net where Susie had wrestled with Jack. And a man sitting on the edge of the steps, cupping his coffee with both hands and looking out at the ocean. There were no screaming people on the rides, no amazing smells of food in the air, no Jack.

The morning walk by the ocean was supposed to help clear Susie's mind and help keep her thoughts off Jack. It was a good plan that failed miserably. Her first mistake was going to a place where she had wonderful memories with the man. Going on the rides. Eating corn dogs. Wrestling in the sand. And the best part, cuddling and kissing toward the end of the evening.

Returning there was a stupid mistake.

She cut short her walk on the beach and headed back up past the Casablanca Inn, around the corner to a cute little coffee place. She ordered a latte and a sesame bagel. Then her thoughts started wandering.

In the direction of Jack.

Maybe she could distract herself with the bagel. She took a bite and chewed slowly. It was toasted with cream cheese, so at least that was one good thing she had going for her. It was delicious, just like her latte.

Susie's thoughts returned to Jack.

Just wonderful.

Was she going to think of Jack every time she thought of coffee, smelled coffee, or saw a Starbucks? For the rest of her life?

"This is a cruel world," Susie mumbled to herself.

"I agree one hundred percent," said a female voice behind Susie. "Very cruel."

Susie set her bagel down and swung around in her chair to get a look at the person who agreed with her.

She was a cute little thing. An older woman. Her Santa Cruz hoodie sweatshirt contrasted with her age, considering she must have been at least seventy years old. Maybe older.

Susie forced a smile. "Good morning."

The woman gave Susie a tsk tsk. "Make up your mind. It's either good or it's cruel. You can't have it both ways."

Susie laughed. "Thanks. I needed that. I'm Susie."

The woman nodded, studying Susie for a few seconds. "I'm Agnes, but my friends call me Aggie."

"Nice to meet you, Aggie. You from around here?"

"I live in Sunnyvale, but I come here just about every weekend. I'm a surfer girl at heart…surfed for over forty years! I'm a legend—ask anyone about Aggie, they'll tell ya."

"I believe you. I don't live that far from you. I'm in Mountain View."

"Practically around the corner from me…"

"Sorry about earlier. I don't usually talk to myself in public and I'm not usually saying the world is a cruel place. Let's just say that last night was not a very good night for me and leave it at that."

"That's okay. I don't really believe the world is cruel. I said that to make you feel better. I'm a pleaser—that's me." Aggie winked and pointed to the empty chair next to her. "Care to join me?"

Susie looked over at the chair. "Oh…"

That was sweet of the woman to offer, but Susie didn't think she would be good company. And she didn't want to share all of her troubles with a complete stranger. No need to ruin someone else's day too.

Aggie waved her off. "Don't worry about it. You can just keep sitting there in your own poop."

Susie laughed again. "I'm quite surprised that I'm laughing, considering the state I'm in." Susie eyed the empty chair again. "Maybe I should take you up on that offer of joining you. You're a miracle worker."

"I don't know about that. I can't give you anything you can't get for yourself."

Susie grabbed her latte and bagel and placed them on the table next to Aggie. "Are you originally from Texas?"

Aggie stared at Susie for a moment. "Do I look like a cowgirl to you?"

Susie laughed again and then covered her mouth. "You need to stop making me laugh. I'm supposed to be sad and heartbroken."

"I apologize. I'll shut up. You can continue being miserable after you tell me why you think I'm from Texas."

"I was researching mascots for a promotion for my business. That's when I found out that an *Aggie* was a student, graduate, or one of the sports teams of Texas A&M University."

Aggie nodded. "Never been to Texas. I was born and raised in California. My parents used to bring me here when I was a child. Always loved it here. Even met my husband here!"

"That's sweet." Susie admired the big diamond on Aggie's finger. "How long have you been married?"

"Would have been fifty-two years this Christmas. He passed last year."

"Oh. I'm so sorry."

Aggie shook her head. "It's okay. If he didn't die from natural causes, I probably would've killed him anyway. Henry was a stubborn, stubborn man." She smiled. "But he was the love of my life." She took another sip of her coffee, the smile continuing to linger on her face. Probably from the memories. "What about you, Susie? Is the world cruel to you because of love problems or is it something work related? I doubt it's your health because you look great."

"Thanks, but I don't want to bore you with my problems."

"Fine with me. Is that poop you're sitting in keeping you warm? Because at the end of the day it's still poop, ya know?"

Aggie was trying to tell her something, but Susie wasn't connecting the dots. What did her problems have to do with poop? Maybe it had something to do with the expression *shit happens*. She tried to piece it together, but couldn't figure it out.

Aggie pointed to her own face. "See these lines on my forehead? They're from thinking too much." She pointed to Susie's face. "You're gonna get 'em if you keep that up."

Susie felt her forehead and tried to smooth away the creases. "Okay…"

"I'll tell ya again…you can sit there in your own poop or —"

"Hang on, Aggie, if you don't mind. Can you explain

this *poop* thing? You make it sound like it's important, but I don't understand what you're trying to say."

Aggie nodded. "Sorry. It's an expression Henry used and I guess I assumed people knew what it meant. Now that I think about it, he had to explain it to me too. What I'm trying to say is...the world gives you complications, right? That's the poop. So, here's the important part—so listen up. Most people complain about the poop, talk bad about the poop, tell the poop to go to hell, say they don't deserve the poop, get depressed about the poop, share the poop with others, you get the idea... But then they do *nothing* about the poop. *They* are sitting in their own poop. Now do you get it? Quit moping around and do something about it. It ain't over 'til it's over or you do something about it. Problems don't get solved by themselves. Do I need to go on? I'm running out of motivation here!"

Susie took in what Aggie had said, and she was right. What was she doing? She had faced her first set of business challenges and then ran away from them instead of trying to figure out a solution. Why did she assume all hope was lost? Maybe that had to do more with Jack than the business. She had high hopes for him and now look what happened. But Aggie was right. It was time to brush that dirt off her shoulder and bounce back. Susie didn't need Jack for that. She was smart enough to get to this point in her life without the help of a handsome man whose kisses almost paralyzed her.

Susie could do it again.

"Why are you still here?" Aggie asked, tapping her fingers on the table. "Go. Get 'er done, girlfriend!"

Susie laughed, standing and clearing her things from the table. "Are you sure you're not a cowgirl?"

"Not even close."

Susie threw her garbage away and turned back. "Thanks, Aggie. You're something special."

Aggie stood and moved toward Susie. "Give me a hug and be good."

Susie gave Aggie a hug and smiled. "Thanks again." Susie pulled a business card from her purse and handed it to her. "This is my place. Please stop by sometime. I would love to treat you to a cup of tea and the best scones in the world. My grandma's recipe and, coincidentally, you remind me of my grandmother."

"It's hard to find good scones. I'll stop by sometime. And I'll look you up on Facebook."

Susie threw her a surprised look. "You're on Facebook?"

"I'm old, but I'm not dead!"

Susie laughed and walked back to the parking lot.

She pulled her keys from her purse and stopped just short of her car, deep in thought.

It didn't make any sense.

Her business had been shut down and the man she was falling in love with had betrayed her, but she had hope. She glanced back toward the coffee place where she had met

Aggie. How did the woman do that? Susie expected herself to be depressed for weeks and now she was ready to go back and deal with her problems.

She smiled and shook her head. "Life isn't cruel. Life is weird."

She slid into her car and turned on her phone. She was surprised it didn't explode from the dings that kept coming and coming from the text messages and voicemails.

She clicked on the most recent voicemail message from Kenneth and listened.

"Where are you? Get your butt down here to the festival. Now! You won't believe what Jack did. Oh. My. God. Gotta go. Anyway, just come. Love you."

Susie stared at her phone.

What had Jack done this time?

Did she really want to know? There was urgency in Kenneth's voice that didn't sound good. Hopefully, everything was okay. She felt guilty for trying to avoid her problems by turning off her phone. She called Kenneth back, and it went straight to his voicemail.

One thing was for sure, she wouldn't sit around there. Something was going on, something not good by the sound of Kenneth's voice, and she needed to head back and deal with it.

Susie drove back over the hill on Highway 17. She tried

to focus on driving safely, but that urge to press hard on the large vertical pedal on the right kept coming.

"Relax. You'll get there when you get there."

Barring any unexpected traffic, it would be forty minutes until she arrived back in Mountain View. Susie felt much better after Aggie's little pep talk in the coffee shop. She needed to make things happen instead of letting them happen to her.

And most importantly...

She wasn't sitting in her own poop anymore.

Chapter Nineteen

Harvey came out of Jack's cafe munching on another scone. "I can't stop eating these things."

Jack wondered how many scones Harvey had eaten so far. Five? Six? "Those are for the customers. You need to have a little self-control."

"I also need to have energy to be the master of ceremonies. These carbs should do just the trick. Hmm. So good."

"Uh-huh…"

Like Jack was going to believe Harvey was just eating the scones for energy. He knew how good they were and eating them had nothing to do with carb-loading, energy, or anything health-related.

Jack smiled as he stared at the throngs of people lining up in front of his cafe behind Harvey. The festival was under way and just about everyone wanted a cup of Susie's tea and one of her scones. He had brought in extra help and Todd got two of their employees to come in and work. Even Alex was back in the scone costume handing out flyers and promising not to brawl with anyone.

Jack felt good.

Everything was going just as planned. He had worked throughout the night, along with Kenneth, Todd, and Harvey to make it happen. It was the right thing to do, and he knew it. It was his fault Susie's place was shut down and Jack had to make it right.

Who knew if Susie would ever forgive him, but he didn't need to think about that at the moment. The goal was to make sure *everyone* talked about her business and to make sure they would come back when she opened again in a few days. Jack had already called in a couple of favors and two electricians were fixing Susie's electrical problems at that moment.

The plan was to get the fire marshal back there Monday morning to give her the okay to reopen. Jack had talked with him and was promised if everything was up to code, she would be able to reopen immediately. No online forms to fill out and mail.

Harvey brushed crumbs off his shirt. "Okay, time to hit the stage."

Jack pointed to Harvey's face. "You missed some...on your chin."

Harvey felt his face with his fingers and found a couple of crumbs on his chin. He stared at them for a second before popping them in his mouth. Then he walked toward the stage.

"Remember what we talked about!" Jack called out.

Harvey turned back. "I'm a professional. Trust me."

As long as Harvey didn't strip again, Jack wasn't worried.

Harvey worked his way up the side stairs of the main stage as Jack admired the street full of people. He loved it when the city of Mountain View shut down Castro Street for these community events. It was a wonderful festival, and he was proud to be a part of it.

"Hello!" Harvey said, waving to two people right below the stage. "I'm Marvy Harvey and we would like to welcome you to another fantastic downtown festival. Before we bring on the band to play some music, I wanted to make a few announcements."

Jack looked on as Harvey thanked the sponsors. He would then make some general announcements about the day's events before talking about Susie's Tea and Scones.

Jack took a deep breath and let it out slowly.

Everything would be okay and maybe one day Susie would forgive him.

Too bad she wasn't there to see what was going on.

The traffic was crazy in downtown Mountain View, which meant Susie had to park ten streets away from the tea shop. She made her way down Castro Street toward the festival. It was amazing how many people were out.

Too bad her tea shop wasn't open.

"Don't go there," she mumbled to herself. "Stay positive."

She walked around the street barricades into the festival. She stopped when she saw a woman walking by eating a scone. Susie looked back and scrunched her eyebrows together.

It looked exactly like one of her scones.

She took a few more steps before she saw another scone coming her way.

Another one that looked exactly like hers.

"Oh my God, these are *so* good," the woman said, taking a bite of the scone. "We need to come back and get more."

Susie had to stop the woman and ask. "Excuse me? Where did you get that scone from?"

The woman pointed down the street behind her and talked with her mouth full. "Hmm. Over there. Hmm. They're amazing. They're from that coffee place on the left. Jack's, right?"

"Yeah," the woman's friend said. "Jack's Coffee Cafe."

Susie tried to keep from blowing a fuse. "Thank you."

What was going on?

Susie's pulse pounded in her neck.

Why was Jack giving away her scones and how did he get them? Based on his past behavior, she wouldn't be surprised if he broke into her shop and stole them.

Susie walked faster, on a mission to find Jack and give

him a piece of her mind.

The nerve.

She picked up her pace as she wove in and out of the people. She approached her tea shop and stopped when she saw the long line in front of Jack's cafe.

Everyone was eating her scones!

Her scones!

She now had to decide. Did she want to make Jack's death fast or slow?

Maybe she'd torture him first.

"Sis!"

Good. Kenneth could help her. This was unbelievable.

She took a few steps toward her brother and pointed to the people all around her eating scones. "What is going on here? How did Jack get my scones?"

"Calm down and give your brother a hug."

Susie hugged him, but she was far from calm. "Seriously, what—" Susie couldn't believe her eyes. She moved toward Jack's cafe and looked through the window. Then she looked back toward her tea shop. "How did all of our furniture get inside Jack's cafe? What is going on, Kenneth?" She braced herself against the newspaper machine, feeling a little weak.

"I told you to calm down."

"Did Jack steal my scones? Or did you figure our business was done, so you gave them all away? I can't believe —"

Kenneth held up his index finger. "Be quiet, Susie."

"The nerve of that man. Somebody needs to—"

"Shut. Up. Now."

Susie stopped talking. She felt lightheaded and continued to lean against the newspaper machine.

"Good," Kenneth said, shaking his head. "Finally. Now look…all of this you see here…" He gestured to Jack's cafe and the people eating scones. "Everything! Was completely planned. And *I* helped. Do you get it now?"

Susie looked around.

No, she didn't get it. She had no idea what was going on. She shook her head, not able to come up with anything intelligent to say.

Kenneth moved closer to Susie. "Do you know what he did for us? Really, for you?"

"Who is *he*?"

Kenneth sighed. "*Jack*. He's not who we thought he was. Not even close. Look!" Kenneth pointed toward the roof of Jack's building. Her Susie's Tea and Scones banner was completely covering his sign. "Jack arranged for electricians to fix our code violations and they're in there right now working on it. He insisted on paying for it. He's not selling coffee today. He's selling our tea. And he's promoting the scones! Look." He handed her a flyer that promoted Susie's Tea and Scones. "He's making sure that every single person at the festival gets one of these flyers. He gave up everything for you, Susie. Everything!"

Susie stood there numb.

How could he do that? Why wasn't he selling coffee? The investors were counting on him to have consistent sales if he wanted any chance of having a national chain. His future was on the line. Why would he throw that all away? He did it for her? Were his feelings as strong as hers? Or was it just guilt?

Susie inhaled deeply and looked around. "Where is he?"

Kenneth turned and pointed toward the stage. "Over there."

Susie turned and spotted Jack and noticed her legs were suddenly moving her body in his direction. She didn't know what she would say or do or how he would react to seeing her. She didn't care. Susie continued to bump into people as she made her way closer to the stage, closer to Jack.

"Okay, just a few more announcements before we bring on the band!" Harvey said from the stage. He paused until the applause died down. "First, we've got free face painting for the kids! Make sure you stop by the booth over in front of the East West Bookstore. Also, every specialty food store and restaurant has free samples today, so make sure you stop by each one of them for a special treat."

Susie could hear Harvey's voice, but her focus, her eyes, were zeroed in on Jack.

The back of Jack's head to be specific.

Then the oddest thing happened.

As if he sensed she was behind him, Jack turned around and locked eyes with Susie.

She stopped walking and swallowed hard.

Her heart was playing some African tribal dance as moisture developed on her palms.

What are you thinking, Jack?

He stared at Susie and she stared right back.

She looked for a sign, something in his body language, an expression on his face to let her know he was happy to see her, that things would be okay. That he was feeling what she was feeling. That they had something special.

Susie wanted him to hold her like he did two nights ago on the beach.

And another kiss would sweeten the deal.

"Jack Robbins, come on up here!" Harvey called, waving Jack to the stage.

Jack opened his mouth like he wanted to say something to Susie and—

Dave Blatt pushed Jack toward the stage. "Get up there!"

Jack turned back to glance at Susie before climbing the stairs to the stage.

Harvey put his arm around Jack. "I want to give a special thanks to Jack Robbins here, owner of Jack's Coffee Cafe, for letting Susie take over his business for the day."

Patience was not Susie's friend that day, but it looked like she would have to wait to speak with Jack.

Jack took the microphone from Harvey. "Thank you, Harvey. Everyone enjoying the festival so far?" More cheers.

"Good—that's what I want to hear. I really wasn't expecting to speak, but I could use this opportunity to thank Susie McKenna, owner of the most amazing tea shop on the West Coast. Her business was supposed to be open today, but there was a mix-up..." Jack paused for a moment, deep in thought.

What was he going to say?

Jack let out a nervous laugh. "Okay, not really a mix-up. Look, I'll be honest with you. It was my fault she's not open—enough said. No need to go into details because frankly, I already feel bad enough. Come on, have any of you ever made a mistake before?" Hundreds of hands went up, including Harvey's. Susie raised her hand too, which caught Jack's attention. "Of course, we've all made mistakes. Anyway, Susie is a special woman and her scones are out of this world! I can see how much everyone is enjoying them, so I want to thank Susie for bringing something amazing to downtown Mountain View."

As everyone cheered, Susie moved closer to the stage, feeling the need—the urge—to be even closer to Jack. Her heart was now pounding in her chest.

"In fact..." Jack pointed to Susie. "Susie's right here. Let's get her up on stage for a few words. What do you say?"

The crowd cheered as Jack gestured for Susie to meet him at the stairs going up to the stage.

Susie shook her head.

Jack waved her up to the stage. "Come on, Susie. You

have fans now and they would love to hear from you. Isn't that right?"

More cheers and applause.

The giant scone came over and held out his hand, escorting Susie up to the stage.

Susie's heart was racing as she approached Jack and took the microphone from him.

She turned toward the crowd and tried to gather her thoughts. She wasn't expecting to be onstage, let alone talking on the microphone.

"Your scones rock, Susie!" a woman yelled from across the street.

Susie smiled and waved to the woman. "Thank you. That means the world to me. My grandmother is no longer with us, but I know she'd be pleased to hear you love the scones since it's her recipe." She admired the people staring at her, many of them still eating her scones. "Funny, but I met a wonderful woman this morning in Santa Cruz who reminded me a lot of my grandmother." She glanced over at Jack. "I met another wonderful person recently. Hi, Jack..." Her voice was barely more than a whisper.

"Hi, Susie. So glad you're here."

"I'm sorry."

Jack jerked his head back. "*You're* sorry? For what?"

"I didn't believe in you. I assumed the worst."

Jack took a step closer to Susie. "*I'm* the one who's sorry. I created this mess and I feel horrible you had to go through it."

She shook her head in disbelief. "I can't believe what you did. You're crazy."

Jack chuckled. "That wouldn't be the first time someone called me that. But everything is going to turn out fine and I hope…" Jack bit his lower lip. "You and me, I hope we're still…something."

Susie wiped her eyes. "I wasn't gone long, but I missed you, as crazy as that sounds. I want us to be something too. I really do."

"Good." Jack smiled, tugging her closer. He wiped a tear from her cheek with his thumb and then pressed his mouth to hers.

The crowd went wild with cheers and whistles.

"Oh my God," Susie said, turning to face everyone. "I totally forgot where we were. This is so embarrassing."

A few laughs and more cheering.

Susie licked her lips. "You taste like scones."

Jack jammed his hands in his pockets and shrugged. "I may have had a few."

Susie laughed. "How many is a few?"

He shrugged again. "Six." He burst into laughter and grabbed Susie's hand, swinging her around like they were ballroom dancing.

She let out a nervous laugh. "What are you doing? Everybody's still watching us."

He shrugged. "Let them watch. I'm just having fun with

you." Jack pulled the microphone from her hand and faced the audience. "Nothing wrong with a little fun, is there?"

The crowd yelled together. "No!"

"See?"

"Life is short!" Harvey yelled, startling both of them. They had forgotten he was still standing right there. "You gotta have fun! In fact, let's get the music started!"

Harvey cued the band, and they started playing "I'm Too Sexy" by Right Said Fred.

"Now you're talking my language," Harvey said, perking up. He stepped forward toward the edge of the stage and undid the top button of his shirt.

The crowd screamed and rushed the stage as Harvey worked on the second button.

Jack covered his eyes and shook his head. "Oh God… here we go again."

Epilogue

One year later…

Susie's Tea and Scones was no longer in business. Neither was Jack's Coffee Cafe.

Jack shook his head, thinking how fast things had changed in the last twelve months.

He stood in the middle of Castro Street, staring back at what used to be both of their businesses.

Now it was just one business.

Jack and Susie had joined forces.

They had named their new place Coffee, Tea or Me.

As expected, the investors had pulled out of Jack's venture after last year's festival. He realized that was the best thing that could have happened. He didn't need to have hundreds of cafes across the country. That meant more work, more stress and no time to have a life.

He wanted to have a life.

A life with Susie.

Initially, Jack wanted to sell Susie's scones in his cafe. Then he thought about how much Susie's furniture was a hit at last year's festival. He sold all the tables and chairs in his cafe and bought new furniture just like hers. Next, they tore down the wall between the two buildings so patrons could go back and forth from one side to another. Jack had gotten the idea while visiting a coffee place nearby. It was connected to a bagel shop, and he loved the idea. So did Susie.

The rest was history.

Jack and Susie continued to stare at the sign on their building.

He grinned and pulled her closer. "Love it."

Susie reached up and kissed Jack on the cheek. "Me too."

They were inseparable and couldn't have been happier —especially since they had gotten engaged six months ago. Jack had proposed to Susie at the Santa Cruz Beach Boardwalk. They'd gone on the Giant Dipper ten times that night, eaten corn dogs, and even wrestled on the beach again. Their wedding was just a month away.

Susie smiled. "Life is funny."

Aggie approached, taking a bite of her scone. "Last year when I met you in Santa Cruz you said life was cruel." She shook her head. "Cruel, cruel, cruel."

Jack turned to Susie. "Did you say that?"

Susie crinkled her nose. "Don't listen to her, she's getting up there in age."

Aggie tapped her temple with her index finger. "There's still *a lot* going on up here. *Who* was the one who beat you in Trivial Pursuit last night?"

"I don't recall," Susie blushed, looking away.

"Of course not. That's because *you're* getting up there in age."

Harvey approached, also munching on a scone. "Ha! I'm older than dirt. In fact, I'm older than the dirt *below* the dirt."

Jack chuckled. "I think that's the earth's crust."

"That's me! I'm crusty. Beat that!"

Aggie inspected Harvey from head to toe. "And *who* might you be?"

Harvey blinked. "I might be Harvey. *Who* wants to know?"

Aggie smiled. "My name is Agnes, but my friends call me Aggie."

"Ahh…the infamous Aggie. Surfer girl. I've heard so much about you." Harvey extended his hand. "A pleasure to finally make your acquaintance."

She accepted his hand. "The pleasure is mine." She held on to his hand a few seconds longer and nodded. "Nice grip."

"Likewise."

Jack glanced over at Susie, wondering if she was thinking the same thing.

Aggie and Harvey were having a moment.

Aggie reached up and squeezed one of Harvey's biceps. "Are these real?"

Harvey winked. "Real as steel."

Oh yeah. Jack was sure he was watching a love connection in the making.

Jack kissed Susie on top of her head. "You're right. Life is funny."

Even Todd was happy. He still worked for Jack and had been dating a woman he had met online. Best of all, the woman had a Tesla and a beach house.

Just the thought of it made Jack smile.

Dave Blatt from the chamber of commerce tapped Harvey on the shoulder. "We need you onstage to thank the sponsors. And don't forget to mention the free balloon animals for the kids."

"Of course. Let me just throw this away." Harvey took a few steps toward the curb, rolled his napkin into a ball, and tossed it in the trash.

Jack couldn't help but stare at Harvey's legs.

"What?" Harvey asked, looking down. "Something wrong?"

Jack grinned. "You have a bounce in your step."

Harvey thought about it for a moment. "Maybe I do and maybe I don't." He winked and turned to Aggie. "You going to be around for a little bit, Aggie? Maybe we could grab a cup of coffee or tea or something. I know a great place nearby."

Aggie smiled. "That's sounds lovely."

"Good."

"Oh…" Dave held up his index finger. "I completely

forgot. Don't forget to introduce the band after you mention the balloon animals."

"You got it," Harvey said, turning and heading to the stage.

Oh no. A band.

Jack yelled in Harvey's direction. "Harvey!"

Harvey stopped and swung around. "Yeah?"

"Promise us you'll keep your clothes on this year."

Harvey flicked the collar of his shirt with his finger. "I'm sorry, but I just can't do that."

THE END
<<<<>>>>

Acknowledgements

Dear Reader,

I would just like to take a moment to thank you for your support. Without you, I would not be able to write romantic comedies for a living. I love your emails and communication on Facebook and Twitter. You motivate me to write faster!

Don't be shy! Send an email to me at rich@richamooi.com to say hello. I personally respond to all emails and would love to hear from you.

It takes more than a few people to publish a book so I want to send out a big THANK YOU to everyone who helped make *Coffee, Tea or Me* possible.

First, thank you to my hot Spanish wife. She's the first person to read my stories and always gives me amazing feedback to make them better. I love you, my angel.

To my cover artist, Sue Traynor, for drawing another incredible cover.

Thanks to Mary Yakovets and Donna Rich for editing and proofreading.

Special thanks to Michael Hauge and Hannah Jayne for the brainstorming sessions.

My beta readers rock! Thank you to Deb, Maché, Robert, and Julita for all you do. You're the best.

Thanks to everyone at the super secret AC author group, Chick Lit Chat, Romance Writers of America, RWA Silicon Valley, Indie Author Collective, and Xanthippe Sterling.

With gratitude from the bottom of my heart.

Rich

P.S. Don't worry, be happy! :)

64888344R00131

Made in the USA
Charleston, SC
08 December 2016